Justis and Eb were buffalo hunters—an ugly pair of an ugly breed. The grins on their faces made them even uglier.

They had reason to grin. They were all set to play their favorite game with the Trailsman. After that, they could play a different game with the woman they had captured.

"We did this with some Arapahos once," Justis said. "We let one go ten yards, then shot her dead. Then we let the next go twenty yards, and did the same. And on and on. Until we had the prettiest row of good injuns you ever did see." He paused. "But since there's just one of you, I'll have to do this a mite different. You head out across that grassland just as fast as you can run. And when we're ready, we're going to start taking pieces out of you a shot at a time until you're on your way to hell. Weave as much as you want, Trailsman. We can blow the eye out of a buffalo at two hundred yards."

Fargo looked at the killers' grins. He saw no mercy there. He looked at the plains in front of him. He saw no place to hide. Skye knew he could run fast—but he didn't see a chance in hell of outrunning a bullet. . . .

ABILENE AMBUSH

THE
TRAILSMAN
144

ABILENE
AMBUSH

by

Jon Sharpe

A SIGNET BOOK

SIGNET
Published by the Penguin Group
Penguin Books USA Inc., 375 Hudson Street,
New York, New York 10014, U.S.A.
Penguin Books Ltd, 27 Wrights Lane,
London W8 5TZ, England
Penguin Books Australia Ltd, Ringwood,
Victoria, Australia
Penguin Books Canada Ltd, 10 Alcorn Avenue,
Toronto, Ontario, Canada M4V 3B2
Penguin Books (N.Z.) Ltd, 182-190 Wairau Road,
Auckland 10, New Zealand

Penguin Books Ltd, Registered Offices:
Harmondsworth, Middlesex, England

First published by Signet,
an imprint of Dutton Signet,
a division of Penguin Books USA Inc.

First Printing, December, 1993
10 9 8 7 6 5 4 3 2 1

Copyright © Jon Sharpe, 1993
All rights reserved

The first chapter of this book previously appeared in *Deathblow Trail*,
the one hundred forty-third volume in this series.

 REGISTERED TRADEMARK—MARCA REGISTRADA

Printed in the United States of America

The Trailsman

Beginnings . . . they bend the tree and they mark the man. Skye Fargo was born when he was eighteen. Terror was his midwife, vengeance his first cry. Killing spawned Skye Fargo, ruthless, cold-blooded murder. Out of the acrid smoke of gunpowder still hanging in the air, he rose, cried out a promise never forgotten.

The Trailsman they began to call him all across the West: searcher, scout, hunter, the man who could see where others only looked, his skills for hire but not his soul, the man who lived each day to the fullest, yet trailed each tomorrow. Skye Fargo, the Trailsman, the seeker who could take the wildness of a land and the wanting of a woman and make them his own.

1860—Abilene . . .
where whiskey and blood
both flowed freely.

1

When a man has a passionate young blonde in a tight red dress perched on his right leg, a full house in his left hand in the form of three kings and two queens, and a pot in front of him totaling over fifty dollars, the last thing he needs is to be distracted from his poker game by someone coming up to him, tapping him on the arm, and saying, "Mister, there's a lady out front who wants to see you."

Skye Fargo frowned as he glanced over his broad shoulder at the stocky bartender. "I don't know any ladies in Abilene," he gruffly responded, and received a playful poke in the ribs from the blonde.

The barkeep shrugged. "Be that as it may, a Miss Walker and some of her friends would like to talk to you." He jerked a thumb at the front entrance, then made for the bar, picking up dirty glasses from various tables along the way.

Fargo idly gazed beyond the batwing doors and glimpsed several women gathered outside in the hot sun. They were all chatting merrily, as if out on a Sunday stroll taking in the meager sights Abilene had to offer. As near as he could tell, every last one was young and on the pretty side. His curiosity was aroused, but he couldn't go talk to them just yet. First he had the pot to win.

"Are you playing or not?" demanded the tall man seated across from Fargo, a grubby sort whose testy nature had been aggravated by his heavy losses during the four-hour poker game. "It's your bet."

"Don't prod me," Fargo warned. The other two players had taken the man's grumbling and sarcastic remarks in stride, but he had tolerated all he was going to. He suspected the others, all locals, were a bit afraid of the tall player, but Fargo wasn't. And he never let anyone ride roughshod over him.

"Then get on with it," the man snapped. "I have more important things to do than sit here and twiddle my thumbs while you make up your mind whether to fold or stick."

An elderly player in homespun clothes coughed lightly and commented, "Ease up, Bell. The stranger ain't taking any longer than the rest of us."

"Did I ask you, Howard?" Bell retorted. "Or do you make a habit out of feeding off your range?"

"I'm not trying to meddle," the old man said.

"Then keep your mouth shut."

Simmering with barely suppressed anger, Fargo slowly counted out ten dollars and added the amount to the pile of money in the center of the table. "It'll cost you to see my hand, Bell," he declared.

The next player folded, and so did Howard, leaving only Bell and Fargo in the game. The former glanced at the pot, then at his cards. He went to shove some of his money out, but hesitated, gnawing on his lower lip.

"What's the matter?" Fargo taunted. "I thought you were in such an all-fired hurry?"

Bell glowered, then impulsively put ten dollars into the pot, leaving a single two-bit coin lying in front of him. "All right. Let's see what you've got, *hombre*."

Fargo gave the blonde a pat on her fanny and motioned with his head for her to stand and move aside. She was smart enough to know that if there was going to be trouble, it would flare in the next few seconds, so she promptly did as he wanted. Fargo, smirking, laid out his cards one at a time, and when he had placed the last queen down, Bell uttered a string of curses and threw his hand to the floor.

"Damn your luck, tinhorn! I have half a mind—"

But Bell got no further, for Skye Fargo had risen, looming over the table with his arms at his sides, his right hand within inches of his Colt, his expression as cold as the icy mask of death itself. His lake-blue eyes glittered as he addressed Bell in a gravelly tone: "Stand up, you son of a bitch, and we'll see which one of us is the tinhorn."

Acting with one accord, the rest of the players vacated their chairs and hastily put themselves elsewhere. Every customer in the saloon had stopped whatever he was doing to witness the confrontation, and a pall of silence had descended.

Now it was Bell's move. He eased his chair backward and

stood, his spine rigid, his body tense for the draw. A wild gleam animated his dark eyes. The left corner of his mouth was contorted by a nervous twitch. Then, at the very moment he seemed about to claw at his revolver, a strange thing happened. He glanced at the bar instead.

Fargo detected motion out of the corner of his eye and, thinking that Bell might have a partner who would throw in with him, turned his head just a fraction and saw a powerfully built man in a fancy brown suit who had an elbow propped on the counter, a whiskey halfway to his mouth, and who was shaking his head meaningfully while fixing Bell with a hawkish stare.

Unexpectedly, Bell licked his lips, looked at Fargo, and straightened. "I don't want no trouble, mister," he said reluctantly, practically choking on the words. "I reckon losing all my money made me shoot off my mouth more than I should. Sorry." Bowing his head, he stepped over to the bar to stand beside the man in the suit.

Puzzled, Fargo studied them. The dandy whispered something to Bell and they both turned away, ignoring him. He wondered what sort of hold the other man had on the hardcase to make Bell back down, but since it was really none of his business, he didn't press the matter. Bending over the table, he scooped up his winnings and crammed them into his pockets.

"How about buying a girl another drink, handsome?" the blonde asked, coming up close to rub her full body against his side.

"In a bit, maybe, Adeline," Fargo said. He polished off his drink, turned, and walked to the batwing doors. Outside, the women still waited. There were five of them, four brunettes and a striking woman with rich black hair, all of whom faced him as he shoved the doors wide and stepped into the bright sunlight. "You wanted to see me?"

"That's right, Mr. Fargo," replied the black-haired woman. She had an oval face with skin as smooth as a baby's bottom and sparkling eyes the color of emeralds.

"How do you know my handle?" Fargo asked, since he had not revealed his identity to anyone since hitting Abilene two days before. He was on his way back to the Rockies after a short stay in St. Louis, and so far as he knew no one was aware he was passing through the territory.

"Is that important?" asked one of the brunettes, a short

woman whose ample bosom swelled her blue dress to the bursting point.

Before Fargo could answer, the black-haired woman asked, "You *are* the man they call the Trailsman?"

"Yes, ma'am," Fargo admitted, studying the whole lot. They were a prim and proper bunch, wearing full-length dresses with high collars and long sleeves despite the blistering Kansas heat. Three of them had their hair done up in buns, while the sassy one and the woman with the raven tresses wore theirs tied at the back with pretty ribbons. Fargo compared them to a church choir without a church. They were as out of place in small but rowdy Abeline as fish out of water.

"I thought so," the black-haired spokeswoman declared happily. "My name, Mr. Fargo, is Susan Walker." She extended her right hand.

Fargo shook, feeling the warmth of her palm against his. She immediately broke the clasp, folded her hands at her waist in a very ladylike fashion, and addressed him.

"Please excuse our boldness in seeking you out, but you're the one man who might be able to help us in our hour of need. That is, if all they say about you is true. You have quite a reputation, Mr. Fargo," Susan said, her rosy lips curling in an odd smile. "It's claimed that you're one of the best guides alive."

"I've been around some," Fargo allowed.

Susan nodded. "Which is why we think you're the man to get us safely to the Rocky Mountains."

Fargo turned to scrutinize Abilene's single dusty street. As towns went, this one was downright pitiful. There was a run-down saloon, an eating house with sleeping rooms attached, a ramshackle livery, a small general store, and several frame houses. A handful of horses were tied to hitching posts, a buckboard sat in front of the store, and at the far end of town, near the livery, were two Conestoga wagons. He thought he understood, and commented, "Oh. You're part of a wagon train. What are you doing so far south of the main trail?"

"We're not with a train, Mr. Fargo," Susan said.

"But those wagons—?"

"They're ours, sure enough, but we're on our way to Mountain City by ourselves."

"Just the five of you?" Fargo blurted, amazed at the revelation. He had heard of harebrained stunts, but this one beat all. "Hasn't anyone told you it's not safe to travel in small parties across the Plains?" he asked. "There are hostiles to worry about, and outlaws everywhere. This is real rough country, ma'am. I'd advise you to go back to Ft. Riley and wait there for the next wagon train that comes along, then join them as far as Denver. You'll be safe that way."

"If we had wanted to take the main trail, we would have," Susan Walker said politely, but with an edge to her voice. "And for reasons of our own we do not care to associate with others at this time."

"It's your life," Fargo said. He pointed at the Conestogas. "But it will take you weeks to reach the mountains, and you have no idea what you're in store for between here and there. Water is scarce, game is almost as hard to find, and every foot of the way you'll have to keep your eyes skinned for war parties and such." He shook his head. "It'd be a miracle if you reach Mountain City alive."

"Which is why we want to hire you," Susan said. "We've pooled our financial resources and can offer you two hundred dollars to guide us across the prairie."

Had Fargo been broke, he might have been tempted to accept the offer. Thanks to his poker winnings, though, he was flush for the time being, and he saw no good reason to risk his life escorting a pack of contrary females across one of the most dangerous stretches of country west of the Mississippi. There were Cheyennes and Kiowas to worry about, not to mention the fact that occasionally the dreaded Comanches ventured into the region on raids. He was doing these women a favor when he replied, "You've come to the wrong man, ladies. I'm not about to get us all killed because you're too stubborn to do what anyone with a shred of common sense would do."

The women exchanged troubled looks. Susan Walker reached out and touched his wrist.

"Please. You don't know how much this would mean to us. We *must* reach Mountain City within three weeks."

"Go back to Ft. Riley. You still might make it in time."

"What if we offered you two hundred and fifty dollars?"

"My answer would still be 'no.' "

The short, sassy one snorted like an angry heifer. "What do you know? The great Trailsman is afraid of a few Injuns and outlaws." She sneered at him. "I should have known. You lousy men are all alike. There isn't one of you worth a tinker's—"

"Danette!" Susan declared. "Remember you're a lady, and ladies do not indulge in vulgar language."

"Sorry, Sue," the other said contritely. "I keep forgetting myself."

"It's obvious we're wasting our time," Susan informed the rest. "Let's not bother Mr. Fargo any longer." Squaring her slender shoulders, she walked off, her hips jiggling enticingly under her dress.

Fargo grinned in amusement as he admired their swaying backsides. Not a one of them, he guessed, was over twenty-five. What in the hell were they doing out in the middle of nowhere all alone? No woman in her right mind would take the gamble they were taking, not when the cost of their foolishness might be their lives. Turning, he reentered the saloon and ambled to the bar. Both Bell and the dandy, he noticed, were gone; they must have gone out the back.

"How about that drink, big man?" Adeline asked, joining him and gluing herself to his left elbow.

Fargo gestured at the bartender for drinks, then inquired of Adeline, "What do you know about those female pilgrims?"

"Not much. They showed up this morning while you were asleep, bought a few goods at the general store, and wandered around getting some exercise. They keep pretty much to themselves. I tried to start a conversation with them as they went by, but they stuck their noses in the air and kept on going, all except the black-haired one. She, at least, had the decency to say hello." Adeline pursed her cherry-red mouth and added, sounding hurt, "Self-righteous types like that bunch don't want to have anything to do with a fallen dove like me."

Their drinks came. Fargo put the women from his mind and let the tonsil varnish burn its way down his throat.

Adeline was doing the same. She winked at him over her glass and polished the whole thing off in three swift gulps. Grinning, she wiped her mouth with the back of her hand and declared, "Practice does make perfect, doesn't it?" She leaned against him and batted her eyelashes. "Now what say we go back up to my room and take up where we left off earlier?"

"I'd like to put some food in my belly first," Fargo said. "I never did have breakfast."

"Oh, yes you did," Adeline responded, reaching up to run a finger under his chin. "In a manner of speaking."

Fargo laughed and took another swallow. He liked Adeline's playful attitude; she was the sole reason he had stayed over in Abilene longer than he'd counted on. A lusty, gutsy woman, she was a regular wildcat under the sheets, as the many fresh scratches on his back proved.

"You know," Adeline commented as if struck by a thought, "someone else was mighty interested in those lady pilgrims, too. Bell and those fellers he's with were asking about them."

About to down the last of his whiskey, Fargo hesitated, oddly bothered by the information. "Bell?" he repeated quizzically.

"Yep. Him and his bunch drifted into town about four days ago. First thing they did was start asking everybody they met if a couple of wagons had been through loaded with women. Bell himself asked me."

"Did he say why they wanted to know?"

"I asked, but he just told me to mind my own business and went off to talk to that handsome, quiet one who dresses real fine. You saw him at the bar. Orland, I think his name is."

"How many were with this Orland besides Bell?"

"Five or six, I reckon. Why?"

"Nothing," Fargo said, although inwardly he was troubled. A hardcase like Bell was bound to be up to no good, and that Orland character had the air of a sidewinder about him. Fargo wouldn't trust either of them as far as he could heave his pinto stallion. They must be fixing to make trouble for those upstanding young ladies, he deduced, which was really none of his affair. But he recalled how desperate the women had been to continue on to the Rockies, and he felt a twinge of guilt over refusing them. "I'll be back in a while," he suddenly announced.

"You going to go eat?"

"I want to check on my horse," Fargo said lamely. He hurried out and turned to the left. The street was deserted except for several chickens scratching in the dirt across the way and a pair of boys playing with sticks at the edge of the prairie. He made straight for the livery. The canvas-topped wagons were still parked where they had been. Both large stable doors hung wide open, but there was no sign of anyone outside or of activity within.

Halfway there Fargo almost changed his mind, worried that he was making a fool of himself. He didn't know these women personally; he had no stake in their welfare. So why should he meddle, especially if he might be wrong and Orland and Bell had a legitimate reason for being interested in them? That thought kept him going. If Orland and Bell were upstanding citizens, then cows could fly.

Fargo slowed as he neared the livery, and loosened his Colt in its holster. His Sharps lay in the room he was sharing with Adeline, but he still had his slender Arkansas toothpick strapped to his right ankle, and in a pinch that could come in mighty handy.

As yet, Fargo had seen no trace of Orland or Bell. But when he was nearly to the front corner of the stable, he happened to glance toward the rear and see the back of a man going around the building. Instantly he changed course and sneaked along the length of the wall. A cautious peek showed him someone crouched at the back door, peering inside. He didn't need to see the figure's face to know who it was. Hooking both thumbs in his gunbelt, he advanced on cat's feet until he was right behind the skulker, and asked, "Lose something?"

Bell's reaction was as lightning-quick as it was violent. Uncoiling, he whipped around and slammed a fist into Fargo's unprotected stomach. Fargo doubled over, the breath whooshing out of him, and felt a second blow connect with his jaw. He staggered backward, saw Bell rise, and clenched his own fists to meet the tall man's rush.

Neither of them made any sound. Like grim gladiators they clashed head-on, Fargo deftly ducking under a vicious swing that would have taken his head off, then planting his own fist smack on Bell's mouth. The tall man grunted and swung again, his knuckles clipping Fargo's shoulder as Fargo evaded the brunt of the blow.

Pivoting, Fargo delivered two swift punches to Bell's stomach that jarred Bell to the spine. Then, blocking a swipe at his face, Fargo drove his right arm up and caught Bell flush on the chin. Bell was sent crashing back against the livery. In a bound Fargo reached him and landed a flurry of solid hits that brought the tall man to his knees.

In desperation, Bell went for his six-shooter.

But Fargo wasn't taken unawares this time. His right knee swept up, striking Bell on the jaw and snapping the man's mouth shut. Teeth crunched, blood spurted, and Bell sagged against the stable. Then, holding Bell's head up with his left hand, Fargo drew his right fist all the way back, paused to relish the moment, and slammed Bell on the jaw again.

Soundlessly, his eyes closed, his shoulders slumped, Bell pitched onto his side.

"You had it coming, you bastard," Fargo said softly. Inhaling deeply, he straightened and stepped to the door, which Bell had opened a crack. Since the tall man would be unconscious for quite a while, Fargo had no fear of being attacked again. He opened the door wide and strode into the cool interior. "Ladies?"

There was no answer. Horses filled many of the stalls on both sides, while to the right was a mound of hay and to the left another mound of straw. In a bin nearby was grain.

"Miss Walker?" Fargo called out.

The women were not even there. Perplexed, Fargo moved down the aisle until he came to the Ovaro. He stopped just long enough to rub the stallion's neck, then he went out the front and surveyed Abilene. Susan Walker and her friends were nowhere to be seen.

Fargo's stomach growled, reminding him of his hunger, and he was on the verge of bending his steps to the eating house when he decided to check in the wagons on the off chance one or more of the women might be resting. The mules paid him no mind. They were dozing in the midday heat, their heads drooping, their long ears flicking as flies buzzed around them.

"Anyone in there?" Fargo asked as he came to the front of the nearest Conestoga. He rapped on the hardwood body, and when there was no response he frowned and went back into the livery. So much for his hunches. Whatever Bell had been up to didn't seem to involve the women at all. But then who had Bell been spying on through the back door? Someone who ran off when the fight started?

Fargo emerged from the building and stopped short, not quite believing his eyes. The tall man was gone! A small circle of drying blood marked where Bell had lain just a couple of minutes ago. He moved forward, his eyes expertly

17

roving over the hard ground, and found a pair of scuff marks. Apparently two men had come along and dragged Bell off.

Fargo followed them, relying on the heel marks left when Bell's heavy boots dragged in their wake. The marks led him along the rear of Abilene's run-down buildings, past the general store, by a picket fence surrounding a frame house, and then to the eating house. Here he slowed, savoring the delicious aroma of roasting steak that wafted through a window. His mouth watered and his stomach rumbled louder than before.

Sighing, Fargo pressed on. He thought for a moment the trail would take him into the saloon, but the drag marks continued westward toward the far end of town. The last structure fell behind him.

A vast sea of gently waving grass stretched into the distance. Fargo halted, pulled the brim of his white hat low against the glare of the harsh sun, and scoured the plain for Bell and the two mystery men. It was as if the earth had split wide and sucked them down, for they were gone. All he saw was a solitary hawk wheeling high on the sluggish air currents.

Frustrated, Fargo turned around and headed for the eating establishment. He wasn't fool enough to follow them out into the open where they could easily pick him off from ambush, not in broad daylight, anyway. Maybe once evening came, he'd mount up and go for a little ride.

Fargo was almost to his destination when he heard the muffled rush of footsteps to his rear. He had just turned into the narrow gap between the picket fence and the eating house on his way to the street, and on hearing them he spun. But he was a shade too slow. A heavy object hammered into the side of his skull, causing him to reel against the wall. Vaguely he distinguished someone clad in brown. Then another tremendous blow blinked out the sun and the sky and the grass and everything, and the last sensation he felt was the rush of air past his falling body.

2

Skye Fargo was gratefully surprised to be alive. He heard the murmur of softly spoken words, impulsively opened his eyes, and promptly wished he hadn't. Waves of agonizing pain flooded through his head. Thunder roared in his ears, in time with the beating of his heart. Wincing, he inadvertently groaned as he blinked and struggled to focus on his surroundings.

"You shouldn't try to move just yet," said a soothing female voice beside him.

A damp cloth was pressed lightly to Fargo's brow. Gritting his teeth against the torment, he looked up into the lovely features of Susan Walker. "You?" he said in surprise.

"Don't talk, either," she admonished. "You have a nasty gash on your head and you've bled quite a bit. If we hadn't found you when we did, you might well have died lying out there in that awful sun."

Slowly the rest of the immediate vicinity crystallized before Fargo's widening gaze. Above him arced a white canvas top, while piled high on either side were personal effects and furniture. "I'm in your wagon?" he mumbled.

"You don't listen very well, do you?" Susan rejoined.

"Men are like that. As stubborn as jackasses."

Fargo had to twist to see the short one, Danette was her name, seated on a padded stool behind Susan. A third woman was framed in the opening, and when she caught him gazing at her she beamed.

"Glad to see you're still with us, handsome. No one has thought to introduce us so I might as well do the honors myself. I'm Audris."

Fargo merely grunted. He didn't feel in the mood for small talk, but he did want some answers. "Who brought me here?" he asked.

"We did," Susan responded, gently wiping his forehead.

"All five of us. We were fixing to leave so we had a bite to eat first. As we came out of the eating place, we heard some sort of commotion coming from around the corner. Danette took a peek and saw you lying there." She paused to dip the cloth in a bucket. "There's no law in this town or we would have notified the marshal. No sawbones, neither. As it was, we had no idea who had done this to you. We didn't know who we could trust. So we just toted you around behind all the buildings and stuck you in here for safekeeping."

On the one hand Fargo was thankful for their help, but on the other he was skeptical. Had it just been coincidence they showed up when they did? And that business about not trusting anyone didn't quite ring true. They could have gone to the owner of the eating house, or the saloon owner, or the livery keeper for help. He stared at Danette and inquired, "Did you happen to see who did this to me when you looked around the corner?"

There was the briefest of pauses. "I heard someone run off but I didn't get a look at him," she answered.

If she was telling the truth, Fargo reflected, then he was Calamity Jane. Rising on his elbows, he grimaced as an acute pang speared through his head.

"And just what do you think you're doing?" Susan demanded.

"I've got to find the bastard who did this to me," Fargo growled. He lifted his right hand to touch his temple, probing until he found the gash she had referred to, a tender spot over three inches long and a quarter-inch deep, just the kind of wound a gun barrel would make. Now he knew how it felt to be pistol-whipped.

"I don't understand why you are in such a rush to go back out and possibly get yourself killed," Susan said crossly. "You're in no shape for a fight. Why not simply rest here for a while until you regain your strength?"

Danette laughed. "Maybe the mighty Trailsman is afraid we bite!"

The comment prompted Fargo to remark, "You never did tell me how you knew who I was. Have I run into one of you somewhere?"

Susan stiffened, caught herself, and forcibly relaxed, adopting a lopsided smile. "No. Of course not. A man like you hardly travels in the same social circles as ladies like us."

"What do you mean by a man like *me*?"

"Well, as I said before, you have quite a reputation."

Fargo didn't believe her for a second, but he was at a total loss to explain why she would lie to him. One fact was clear, however. There was more to these women than they let on. For such an innocent-acting bunch, they hid more secrets than politicians. He slowly sat up, spotted his hat, and carefully eased it onto his head.

"You're a damn fool, Skye Fargo," Susan declared. "You don't know when to leave well enough alone."

"Can't be helped. I've always been an ornery cuss," Fargo responded. "And I never have been willing to turn the other cheek. Whoever did this to me is going to wish he'd picked on a grizzly instead." Bracing a hand on the blankets underneath him, he shoved up into a crouch and made for the front of the wagon.

"Is there any chance you've changed your mind about guiding us to the Rockies?" Susan wanted to know.

"No."

"Who needs this grump?" Danette interjected. "I say we keep going by ourselves. We've come this far without any problem. We can make it the rest of the way."

Fargo climbed onto the seat beside Audris, who gave him the sweetest little grin, and turned to lower himself to the ground. He stopped in surprise on observing the other two women standing next to the mules, each with a rifle in her arms. "Expecting company?" he said as his boots touched down.

"Abilene doesn't appear to be a very safe town," said the younger of the pair, with a meaningful glance at his temple.

"You be careful, mister," said the other impishly. "We wouldn't want anything else to happen to you."

They both giggled.

Fargo had met some mighty peculiar females in his travels, but he had to admit he'd never met any quite like this group. Evidently they were all from different sections of the country. The young one had a distinct Eastern accent, the other a hint of a Southern drawl. Audris was harder to pin down, but Fargo would lay odds she'd been born east of the Mississippi. Susan Walker and Danette, however, both spoke as if born and bred in the West. What had brought them all together?

"Do come visit us again, Mr. Fargo," the young one said.

Fargo paused. "You're one up on me, ladies. Mind telling me your names?"

"I'm Catherine," revealed the young one, and winked. "My friends all call me Cathy."

"Call me Rita," said the last woman, and somehow she managed to speak those three words as seductively as any ever spoken in the English language.

From the wagon came a stern rebuke. "Ladies! Remember who you are now! What would they think?"

"Don't get on your high horse again, Sue," Catherine replied indignantly. "We're not there yet, are we? What harm can it do?"

Sue Walker had her hands on her hips and a flush of color in her lovely cheeks. "You know damn well what could happen. We've been all through this so many times I'm sick to death of having to remind you how to behave. We all agreed, Cathy. If one of us falls by the wayside, she gets left behind." Her tone became edged with steel. "Is that what you want to do? Go back?"

Fargo saw the young woman blanch as might someone who had just confronted a ghostly specter. She gulped, shook her head vigorously.

"No! Never! Not so long as I draw a breath. I'm sorry, Sue. It won't happen again."

Fargo was more mystified than ever. The woman's terror was the genuine article. But what did she have to be so afraid of? He glanced up at Sue and found her eyes on him.

"Since you've spurned our aid, Mr. Fargo, you might as well be on your way. But keep in mind we'll be leaving in the morning, westward as we originally planned. If you should decide to accompany us after all, you know where to find us."

With a touch of his hat brim, Fargo departed. His first stop was the eating house where he took a seat in a far corner, his back to the wall, and ordered a heaping portion of steak and potatoes. He had the biscuit-shooter bring him a cup of steaming black coffee and went through four refills before the meal arrived.

As Fargo wolfed his tasty food and gulped down the hot brew, he pondered the string of events since his initial meeting with the five women and tried to make some rhyme or reason out of the incidents. He remembered the glimpse he'd had of a figure in brown just before he'd been battered unconscious, and he recalled that the dandy at the bar, Orland, had worn an immaculate brown suit. Had it been him? If so, why? Because of the thrashing Fargo had given Bell? Just what in hell had he gotten himself mixed up in, anyway?

The food and coffee did wonders for Fargo's constitution. Most of the pain abated. He stepped from the eatery feeling brand new, and walked down the quiet street to the saloon. The usual bunch were playing cards or drinking or huddled together talking. Adeline was at the bar with another of the women who worked there, and she broke off and hurried over as soon as she saw him.

"I was beginning to think you'd rode out without saying good-bye," she declared. "What took you so long?"

Fargo lifted his hat a few inches, exposing the gash.

"Jesus, Mary, and Joseph! How did that happen? You try to shoe a horse with your head?"

"Some sidewinder jumped me," Fargo answered, and elaborated just enough to provide the basic details. "Have you seen Bell or Orland in here since I left?"

"Nope. Neither one. Do you figure it was one of them?"

"Could have been anyone," Fargo said, and let the matter drop. Adeline was a terrific partner in the sack, but the rest of the time she tended to let her gums flap more than they should. If he flat-out told her he was after Orland, everyone in Abilene would have heard the news by morning.

"Do you know what you need?" Adeline asked, gliding next to him and pressing her ample cleavage against his arm. "Rest. Lots and lots of rest. So why don't we go to my place and I'll nurse you back to health?"

"We might as well," Fargo said. He didn't have any other plans, not until after sunset, at least. Looping his arm in hers, he escorted her out and over to the room she rented adjacent to the eating house. She removed the key from her bag and bent over to insert it into the lock, her shapely buttocks jutting upward inches from his groin. Whether by design or not, the pose stimulated Fargo's imagination and he thought of the last time they had made love, of her lush, naked body, of her firm, rosy nipples. Unbidden, his

23

manhood twitched, then hardened and rose, straining against his buckskins.

Fargo restrained his passion as they both stepped inside and he closed the door. Adeline was tossing her bag on the bed. In a stride he was behind her, his body molded to hers, his hands cupping her breasts while his manhood ground into her rear end.

"My goodness! Ain't you the randy one."

Her perfumed neck beckoned Fargo's lips. His hands roamed up and down her body, from her throat to her pubic mound, massaging every square inch. In a while she vented a contented sigh and began to grind herself against him. The junction of her thighs became warm to the touch, even through the material of her dress. When he pressed there with the tips of his fingers, she squirmed and cooed.

"I can never get enough of you, big man."

Fargo steered her to the edge of the bed, then slowly turned her around until their mouths locked. Her tongue snaked out, entangled with his. Her left hand closed lightly on his organ and she moaned deep in her throat. He commenced unfastening her dress. Soon her garments were strewn at his feet.

Lowering her onto her back, Fargo stripped off his hat and shirt. In his lust he forgot about his wound and jerked his head when he accidentally brushed the shirt against it. Tossing the shirt aside, he clamped his mouth on her left breast, tweaking the stiffening nipple, while his hand gave her right breast a similar treatment.

"Ummmmmm, yes," Adeline husked.

Ever so lightly, Fargo traced a path across her flat stomach, through her crinkly hair, to her moist slit. His forefinger descended, parting her hot nether lips, and he swirled the finger around in her tunnel.

Adeline, her eyes closed, arched like a cat and clasped his arms tight. "Never get enough!" she repeated, lost in ecstasy. "Never get enough!"

Fargo knew how she felt. He stroked her, slowly at first but with increasing intensity, and she moved her hips to accommodate his thrusts, timing her movements so that she was driving her hips downward as his finger stabbed upward. His palm grew slick with her juices.

"Uh! Uh!" Adeline panted.

His manhood pulsing, Fargo tugged at his pants and got

them down around his knees. Her fingers enfolded the tip and stroked knowingly, threatening to bring him to the brink much sooner than he wanted. To take her mind off his pole, he inserted two fingers instead of one into her wet core and rammed them both in as far as the knuckles.

"Aaaaaeeeeeee!" Adeline squealed, bucking like a wild mustang. Her teeth sank into his shoulder, drawing blood, and her fingernails raked his back, opening fresh cuts.

Unfazed, Fargo took hold of her right breast and squeezed. She thrashed, her legs pumping convulsively, her buttocks humping up off the bed. His fingers slid from her womanhood and were replaced by the tip of his burning organ. Then, inch by gradual inch, he fed himself into her.

"Dear Lord! You're so huge!"

Now Fargo held still, relishing the exquisite sensation of being inside her. Her nails gouged his biceps and she squirmed under him, heightening his pleasure. Her tongue lathered his ear. He commenced a stroking motion, slowly so as to prolong their lovemaking. The bed squeaked under them in time to the tempo of their movements.

Time became irrelevant. Fargo gave no thought to anything except the lush body he was fondling and kissing. Adeline took to panting like a steam engine about to jump its track. Her hands were everywhere; she couldn't seem to get enough of his powerful, hard form.

Presently Adeline stiffened, her mouth shaped into a delectable oval, and declared, "Oh! Oh! I'm almost there!" Her body trembled. She bit him again. Then, uttering a sharp cry, she pounded into him with a fury, gasping at each lunge, taking herself over the edge. A low moan filled the room.

Fargo waited until he felt the wet walls of her tunnel constrict around him and heard her gasps of rapture, then he rose on his knees and rammed into her to the hilt, over and over again, allowing his pent-up passion free rein. An explosion built at the base of his organ and pulsed outward. He cried out himself when he spurted into her, and he kept on spurting and pumping until he couldn't do either any more. Drained of all energy, he slumped on top of her twin mounds and pecked her cheek.

"Big man, you are marvelous," Adeline said.

Fargo made no comment. His head was starting to hurt again, thanks to his exertion. He touched his temple and noticed a tiny drop of blood on the end of his finger when he pulled his hand away.

"You all right, lover?"

"It's nothing a little rest won't cure," Fargo assured her, rolling onto his back. He stretched out, draped a forearm over his eyes, and tried not to dwell on the growing discomfort. At length he dozed, Adeline cozy and warm at his side.

Pain awakened Fargo, or so he thought at first. He lay there in the subdued light and realized they had slept until evening. The room had grown stuffy so he decided to open the window and let some air circulate, but as he slipped his right leg over the side of the bed his ears registered the faintest of sounds from the direction of the door.

Instantly Fargo's senses were primed. The sound, a metallic scratching, was repeated. He saw that the knob was turning a fraction of an inch at a time as whoever lurked in the hall tried to open the door without alerting Adeline or him. Whoever it was must figure they were both asleep, he reasoned. Perhaps their visitor had been listening and heard snoring.

Fargo didn't care to be caught with his britches down. Easing away from Adeline so as not to arouse her, he stood and hiked his pants around his waist, then quickly grabbed his gunbelt and strapped on the Colt. Drawing it, he padded over behind the door and waited to surprise the intruder.

The surprise was on him.

Suddenly the door swept inward, crashing into Fargo and slamming him back into the wall. The Colt was jolted from his fingers. A burly man in a flannel shirt and jeans leaped around the edge of the door and leveled a revolver. Fargo jerked aside as the gun boomed, then he pounced, swatting the barrel aside before the man could fire again. His right fist caught the man on the mouth and propelled him into the bed, where Adeline had sat up with a yelp.

Tensing his leg muscles, Fargo leaped, his arms outstretched. He landed on the would-be assassin as the man tried to rise and got a grip on the killer's gun arm. Locked together, each trying to gain the upper hand, they rolled to the left, off the foot of the bed, and onto the floor.

Fargo wound up on the bottom. A knee was jammed into his midriff, lancing agony through his ribs. He used his own knee, driving it up between the killer's legs, and was rewarded with a gurgle of anguish. Applying leverage, he flipped his adversary to one side.

Adeline was demonstrating the remarkable vitality of her lungs by bawling for help so loudly they could probably hear her clear in Dallas.

The assassin, growing desperate, unexpectedly butted Fargo with his head, striking Skye's wounded temple. Fargo's consciousness swirled, and for a few seconds he feared he would pass out. His grip on the gunman involuntarily relaxed. The killer, taking advantage, yanked loose and scrambled to his feet, evidently intending to flee before others could arrive on the scene. He'd taken a single stride when he was pelted from behind by a heavy pillow heaved by Adeline.

Fargo saw the burly man trip over his own feet and fall to one knee. Before the assassin could rise, Fargo hurled himself at the man's back. He encircled the killer with both of his brawny arms and smashed the man down onto the floor. The revolver went skidding off across the smooth floorboards, so now they were evenly matched.

Not about to give up, the killer lashed backward with his boots, raking Fargo's legs with his spurs. Fargo felt a sharp stinging in his right shin. Releasing his hold, he pushed to the right and rose in a crouch. His right hand darted to the top of his boot, his fingers flicked inside for the hilt of his Arkansas toothpick.

Only the knife wasn't there!

Fargo had no time to wonder what could have happened to it. The killer was on him the very next moment, swinging fists as hard as rocks, trying to batter him senseless. Backpedaling, Fargo blocked a few punches, ducked under others, then set his legs and refused to retreat any further. His right fist lifted the man off the floor. His left sent the assassin tumbling.

With a start, Fargo saw the burly man fall within two feet of the revolver. He knew the killer would scoop up the gun; he knew he couldn't stop him. So instead of charging the man, Fargo turned and raced to where his Colt lay. He took a running dive as the killer twisted to seize the revolver. His body crashed down, his frantic fingers closed on the six-shooter. In his ears boomed the retort of the killer's gun and a heavy slug tore into the wall above his head, causing wood chips to rain on his face. Spinning on his stomach, Fargo snapped off a shot.

A reddish hole blossomed between the burly man's eyes as his head snapped back and his mouth fell open. He blinked once, then sprawled onto the floor with a thud.

Just like that, it was over. Fargo slowly rose and walked over to study the killer's features.

"Anyone you know, handsome?" Adeline asked.

"Never laid eyes on the son of a bitch before," Fargo answered. Out in the hall there were yells and rapid footsteps. He swiftly replaced the spent cartridge, then trained the Colt on the doorway as a skinny man wearing spectacles appeared.

"My goodness," the newcomer exclaimed on seeing the corpse. He nervously rubbed his hands together and shifted his weight from foot to foot. "This is terrible!"

"What kind of place are you running here, Rice?" Adeline snapped angrily. "A lady can't even take her rest without some hardcase trying to do her in."

The proprietor's shock evaporated and he glared at her. "You're not—" he began testily, but prudently changed his mind when she grabbed at the other pillow. "That is," he hastily corrected himself, "I doubt you were the one in danger. You've boarded here for months now and never given me cause for complaint." His gaze shifted to Fargo. "I'd guess that poor soul on the floor was after your, uh, gentleman friend."

Fargo twirled the Colt into his holster and finished dressing. This made the third attack on him since he'd met those five women earlier. There had to be a connection. He remembered Adeline saying that there were about a half-dozen men with Orland, which led him to suspect the polecat on the floor must have been one of them. But why had they tried to murder him in his sleep? Was it Bell's handiwork? As he straightened and pulled his hat down over his forehead, his mouth tightened in a grim line. He was damn tired of being a target. Someone was going to give him some answers or there would be hell to pay.

3

Skye Fargo's first stop was at the pair of Conestogas. They sat quiet and dark in the gathering gloom, and not surprisingly, no one was there. He checked the livery but saw only the proprietor sipping a flask at the back. "Old-timer!" he called out. "Any idea where the women who own the wagons got to?"

The proprietor reacted as if he'd been jabbed with a pitchfork and nearly dropped his flask. His hands shook as he turned and jabbed a bony finger at the Trailsman. "Don't be creepin' up on folks like that, you darned dunderhead! You about made me die of fright."

"What's got you so jumpy?" Fargo asked.

"Nothin'. I don't want no trouble. I'm a peaceable man, always have been. And I'm too old to change my ways." He sniffed, then took a long sip. "Now what was it you were wantin'?"

"I need to know if you've seen the women who own the wagons," Fargo said, gesturing over his shoulder.

"Sure, I've seen 'em. Sometimes they're there and sometimes they ain't. But I don't keep track of every move they make. Think I care to follow them to the outhouse? I should say not, not at my age." He took another sip. "What makes you think they tell me anything, anyway? I never said that. And I'll deny it if you claim I did. You're barkin' up the wrong tree, mister. Now go away and leave me alone. I got work to do."

Thinking that half the population of Abilene was touched in the head, Fargo frowned in disgust and went to leave when the full significance of the proprietor's words hit him. He headed down the center aisle. The man had already turned away and was gulping the bug juice as if each swallow would be his last. Consequently, he had no idea Fargo was still there until Fargo's hand fell on his shoulder.

"Jesus!" the proprietor declared, whirling so fast he spilled some of his precious whiskey. His face became livid. "Didn't I just tell you not to do that? What the hell is the matter with you? Do you have wax in your ears?"

"Where are the women?"

"If you don't beat all. I have half a mind to—"

Fargo had no inclination to bandy words, not after all that had happened to him. His left hand shot out and seized the front of the old man's faded shirt. "I won't ask again, old-timer. Tell me where the women are or I'll take that flask and break it over your head."

The man's face paled to a sickly white and he gulped. "Now hold on, young fella. I didn't mean to rile you. But like I said—"

"I want the straight truth," Fargo warned, and gave the proprietor a shaking that made the man's teeth chatter. "They told you something and I want to know what it is."

"I don't want to get involved. *Please,* mister. Let me go and forget about this. They'll kill me if I spill the beans."

Fargo relaxed his grip. "Who will?"

"That jasper Orland and his outfit. They're mean, sidewinder mean, and they don't care who they rub out."

Twisting, Fargo surveyed the dark street outside, then he clutched the proprietor's thin arm and drew the man into a nearby empty stall where they were shrouded in shadow. "No one can see us or hear us. Talk fast."

Anxiously licking his lips, the man glanced all around, scowled, and hunkered down, motioning for Fargo to do likewise. "All right," he whispered. "You'll likely get me killed, but I can't stand to think of what will happen to all those pretty ladies if somebody doesn't do something." He upended his flask, capped it, and stuffed it into a back pocket. "Here's all I know. The first day those ladies showed, the one with the black hair took me aside and told me to let her know if any strangers came around asking about them. She claimed there were some men on their trail."

Fargo thought he heard a scratching sound from beyond the open doors, but when he looked he saw only the vague outline of the mules, which were still in harness. Suddenly he realized the mules had been kept that way all day, as if the women were prepared for a quick getaway if need be.

"I should have told her about Orland, but I didn't," the

old-timer was saying. "His bunch came into town a few days before the gals did, and he came into my place wanting to know if a couple of Conestogas had been by, headin' west."

"Why didn't you let Miss Walker know?"

"Because that Orland fella had made it plain he'd be real displeased if the women should show and I told. He was fingerin' his belly gun when he threatened me, and the way his eyes glittered was downright spooky. I decided right then and there I didn't want no part of that bunch."

"Did everyone in town know Orland was interested in those women?"

"Oh, sure. He told Rice over to the eating house, Weaver over to the saloon, and most everybody else. And he warned them to keep their mouths shut just like he warned me. Then him and his men just settled down to wait."

Fargo now understood why the men involved in the poker game had been so scared of Bell. Orland's gang had the whole town cowed. All except feisty Adeline. He was beginning to suspect that her mention of Bell's interest in the women had been more than a casual comment. She must have wanted him to get involved, to lend Susan Walker and her friends a hand, and that had been her way of sparking his interest.

"I was a mite surprised when those wagons did show," the proprietor had gone on. "I mean, it isn't every day you see a passel of women traveling alone across the prairie. And such young, pretty things at that. For a while I was afeared Orland and his men would harm them, but he didn't lay a finger on them. Fact is, him and his bunch started actin' almighty peculiar. They hid out in the saloon or their rooms all the time as if they didn't want the women to know they were in Abilene."

"So the women never caught on?"

"Not until late this afternoon. That Walker woman looked me up and wanted to know if anyone fittin' Orland's description had been around. Well, I tried to do as Orland wanted and not let on, but as you noticed I ain't much of a liar. Never did have the knack. She knew without me sayin' a word."

"How did she act?"

"Real calm. But I could see she was worried. Her and the others had a palaver out by the wagons, and some were sayin' they should go on right away while Walker and the short one with the mouth were sayin' they should stay until mornin' in case some fella named Fargo decided to help 'em." The old man paused. "Say, that wouldn't be you, would it?"

"It would."

"Then I'll take this as an omen."

"A what?"

"An omen to show me what to do. I was tryin' to make up my mind whether to get all the menfolk in town together and try to convince them to go help those gals when you moseyed in. Now you can go."

"Go where?"

"There's a gully about half a mile west of town. For some reason Orland had a couple of his men set up camp there. I never would have knowed if I hadn't been out hunting and saw the smoke from their campfire. Naturally, I went over to have a look-see."

Fargo straightened. "You think the women are there?"

"I know they are. About half an hour ago, when I was busy cleanin' out the stalls, three of Orland's men came through my livery from the back. I ducked down and they never saw me, but you can believe I saw the hardware they were totin'. They took the ladies by surprise. Covered 'em from just inside the door and told them if they shouted for help the lead would fly. Then they had those gals march on in here and took them out the back way."

Fargo had heard enough. He hurried to the Ovaro, led the stallion from the stall, and grabbed his saddle blanket.

"Listen, mister," the proprietor said, coming over. "I don't want you thinkin' poorly of me. I'm not a coward. But I'm not a fool, neither. I couldn't buck odds like that."

About to pick up his saddle, Fargo glanced at the old man and saw the inner torment mirrored in his eyes. He also saw the light from the lantern glinting off the top of the flask. "It's a smart man who knows when to play a hand and when to fold," he responded.

"Thank you," the proprietor said softly.

It took but a minute and Fargo had the pinto saddled. Stepping into the stirrups, he turned toward the entrance. The old-timer's voice stopped him.

"You be mighty careful, young fella. It's been my experience that any *hombre* who wears his hardware tied down ain't one for doing much talkin' with his mouth. And that

Orland character carries his tied down under his jacket high on the left side. Favors a cross-draw. You can't even tell it's there to look at him."

"I'm obliged," Fargo said. He touched his spurs to the Ovaro's flanks and rode to the eating house. Adeline wasn't in the room. Draping his saddlebags over his shoulder, he picked up his bedroll, retrieved the heavy Sharps, and went out.

Coming down the hall toward him was Rice. The skinny man noted the gear, then asked with a hopeful smile, "Are you leaving us, perchance?"

"Figured I'd sleep out on the prairie tonight," Fargo responded. "At least there I won't have bedbugs eating me alive and keeping me up all night." He shouldered past the flabbergasted owner.

"Bedbugs!" Rice sputtered. "What are you talking about? I'll have you know I keep a clean place! No one has ever complained of vermin before."

Fargo halted at the door to look back. "I wouldn't worry about it if I was you. Bedbugs are fairly common. But I'd take care of your mouse problem before word gets around or no one will ever want to stay here."

"Mouse problem?" Rice repeated in horror.

But Fargo was already outside and shoving the Sharps into the boot. In due course he had his saddlebags and bedroll strapped on and, gripping the horn, he swung up. Abilene was its usual sleepy self as he trotted westward to the end of the dusty street, where he abruptly slanted to the left. A cool breeze from the northwest brought welcome relief after the oppressive heat of the day. On all sides the tall grass swayed and danced. To the east the pale moon was rising.

A wide loop brought Fargo up on the gully from the south. It was easy enough to find; the flickering glow from the fire marked the exact spot and was visible for a mile or better. Orland was making no effort to hide, which showed he wasn't the least bit concerned about the good citizens of Abilene interfering with whatever he was up to. But the man wanted privacy or he wouldn't have had the women brought out to the isolated gully.

Approximately a hundred yards from the fire, Fargo drew rein, dismounted, and ground-hitched the Ovaro. Shucking the Sharps, he fed a cartridge into the chamber, then stole silently forward through the whispering grass. The orange glow blinked on and off as figures moved about, and faint, muted voices wafted toward him on the breeze.

When Fargo was thirty yards away he dropped into a crouch, held the Sharps in front of him, and worked warily along until he came within twenty feet of the south end of the gully. It wasn't much higher than the height of an average man and open at the end he faced, so he had an unobstructed view of everything taking place. And what he saw added to his perplexity.

Orland was present, all right, as was Bell and six other men. Evidently Adeline had not seen all of the gang. Most of the men were lounging at ease or strolling about in the confined space. Bell sat close to the fire, the bruises and contusions on his face starkly obvious in the glare of the crackling flames. Well past the fire, nearer the north end of the gully, sat Orland in earnest conversation with Susan Walker. The rest of the women were scattered about, and every last one was chatting with one or two of Orland's men as if they were the best of friends. Not a single member of the gang was holding a gun on the ladies. Not a single woman was bound. There was no evidence whatsoever that they were being held against their will.

Fargo began to doubt the women were in any danger at all. They were all talking so softly he couldn't hear the words clearly, but from the look of things, Orland's men and the ladies knew each other quite well. But if so, why the secrecy on Orland's part? Why had he threatened the people of Abilene with violence if they told the women he was in town? And why had Walker told the livery proprietor that certain men were after her and the others? None of it made a lick of sense.

After watching for nearly ten minutes, Fargo figured he had made an idiot of himself and he might as well return to Abilene. He twisted, eased backward, then froze.

The man called Orland had suddenly stood and uttered a string of harsh oaths. His right hand swept in a savage arc, catching Susan Walker on the cheek and knocking her to the ground. Danette and Audris started to go to her aid when one of the men whipped out a six-shooter and leveled it at them.

"That'll be far enough, gals!"

Fargo needed to hear more so, tucking the Sharps next

to his body, he crawled close enough to catch every word. Orland was speaking, addressing Susan.

"—think you can do this to me and get away with it? And here I thought you had brains enough to recognize how things are and to know you can't change it." Orland made an exasperated gesture. "If I was the bastard you make me out to be, I'd have you killed right here and now. But I won't. Instead, I'm taking you back, and you'll take up where you left off."

Susan had a hand to her face, but she wasn't cowering in fear. Her features radiated defiance, and her next words were spat out. "We'll never go back!"

"Care to bet?" Orland countered. "I didn't come all this way to return empty-handed. Your little stunt has cost me a lot of money and time, and I aim to collect both once we're home."

"Home?" Susan cried. "How can you dignify that pit with such a title? It's no more a home than a slaughterhouse would be, except that the cows who go to their slaughter don't have a choice. We do."

"Don't start again. You'll only get me riled."

"And what will you do? Beat me? Cripple me like you did Martha Danbridge?"

"How many times are you going to keep carping on her? I didn't mean to break her spine. She fell wrong, is all."

"You were the one who sent her tumbling down the stairs."

"And I'd do it again to her or anyone else who insults me the way she did. Martha was a hothead, Sue. You know that. She was forever running off at the mouth. Like you, she didn't have enough common sense to fill a thimble."

Susan Walker lowered her arm and rose to her knees. "We won't go back, Tom, no matter what you do to us. We can't be intimidated any more."

"Is that so?" Orland said blithely. He glanced at his men, some of whom cackled, then abruptly took a half-step and belted Susan across the mouth, crumpling her in a heap at his feet. "My patience is at an end, bitch. It's time you learned some manners and I'm just the gent to teach them to you." Pivoting on his heel, he walked to the west side of the gully where the horses stood and opened a saddlebag on a zebra dun.

Fargo craned his neck to see the object Orland was removing, but the man's back was to him and he couldn't tell what it was until Orland had turned completely around. Clasped in Orland's right hand was a bullwhip, which he cracked in the air with a smooth flick of his wrist.

"No!" Danette cried, and took a stride toward him. The hardcase with the pistol in his hand gave her a rough shove and she stumbled back against the east wall of the gully. "You don't listen too good, do you, bitch?" he taunted.

"Bell!" Orland snapped. "Quit sitting there like a bump on a log and earn your keep. Line up the others and make damn sure they don't interfere."

The tall man sighed and rose. His right hand draped on the butt of his six-gun, he strolled over and motioned at the rest of the women. "You heard the man, ladies. Get over here and behave yourselves."

"Bell, you can't let him do that to her," Danette said.

"Mr. Orland can do as he damn well pleases," Bell replied. "In case you've forgotten, he owns you lock, stock, and barrel. He could kill you and I wouldn't lift a finger."

"And I thought you had a shred of decency in you!" Danette said.

"Why, kitten, whatever gave you such a harebrained notion?" Bell responded, eliciting mirth from several of his companions.

Fargo's teeth clenched. He wasn't about to lie idle while Orland peeled Susan Walker's fair skin off with that bullwhip. Staying flat, he worked his way to the right, stealthily creeping through the buffalo grass until he reached the east side of the gully. Here he angled upward, staying close to the rim but not so close as to expose himself to the men below. As he crawled he could hear everything being said.

Orland gave a short bark of a laugh. "I'm going to enjoy this, Sue. I should have done it ages ago. I probably would have saved myself a heap of grief."

"If that lash touches me, I'll kill you," Susan Walker vowed in a low tone.

"You'll never get the chance," Orland said, and the bullwhip cracked again, louder than before. "And you should know better than to threaten me, dearest. Nothing makes me madder."

"Think I care?"

"You will by the time I'm through with you. Believe me, you will."

Fargo judged he had traveled far enough. Orland and Susan must be right below him, while the other women were in a row to his left and Bell and the six gunmen stood in front of them. From his vantage point he would be able to cover every member of the gang at once. Easing the Sharps to his waist, he cocked the hammer, then lightly pulled the rear trigger to set the front trigger so that the merest tap would cause the rifle to fire. This hair trigger, as it was called, gave him a fraction of an instant's edge in a gunfight.

The bullwhip snapped again, sounding like the retort of a derringer.

Taking a breath, Fargo steeled his muscles, then rose to his knees and tucked the Sharps to his right shoulder, the barrel trained squarely on Orland's chest. "That'll be enough!" he thundered.

Tom Orland was in the act of lifting his bullwhip high. He went rigid, his face betraying his shock. In front of him, the shoulder of her dress shredded, crouched Susan Walker. She glanced around, her joy transparent.

Fargo spoke again quickly before any of Orland's dumb-founded men could recover their wits. "If one of you so much as twitches, I'll blow your boss's head off."

The gunman with the pistol ignored the warning and went to raise his gun arm.

"No!" Orland bellowed. "You holster that piece, Clancy, and do as the man says."

"But—" Clancy protested.

"Do it, you damn fool!" Orland roared. "Or I'll kill you myself! That's a Sharps he's holding, boy, and it puts a hole in a man the size of a melon. Put your six-shooter away, now!"

Exhibiting a marked unwillingness to comply, the young gun-shark nevertheless obeyed, jamming his pistol into its scabbard with a defiant flourish. "There! Satisfied?"

"I'm not," Fargo stated gruffly. "I want all of you to unbuckle your gunbelts and let your hardware drop."

"Like hell I will!" Clancy responded arrogantly.

Fargo wanted to avoid a gun battle if he could. He was hopelessly outnumbered, and should they all go for their guns at once, one of them was bound to get him before he could possibly drop them all. Worse, some of the women might be accidentally hit in the crossfire. But he was beginning to think he would have to shoot the hothead in the hope of getting the rest to fall into line when he received help from an unexpected source.

Bell was standing next to young Clancy, his arms draped at his sides. Suddenly, without warning, his right fist swept up and crashed into Clancy's chin, dropping the young man in his tracks. Then, his arms outspread so Fargo could see he was not trying some sort of trick, Bell bent down and gingerly plucked Clancy's pearl-handled Colt out with two fingers and tossed the revolver to the ground.

"I reckon I was wrong about you," Fargo said. "I didn't know you could be so reasonable."

"There will be another day, another time," Bell said, as he unfastened his own gunbelt and let it fall.

Fargo watched out of the corner of his eye as the rest imitated the tall man's example. Then he concentrated on Tom Orland. "The whip and your gun, too."

Calmly, almost disdainfully, Orland threw the bullwhip into the grass. "I don't carry a six-shooter," he remarked. "Never have been much of a shot."

"Is that a fact?" Fargo rejoined, remembering the old-timer's advice. "I suppose you won't mind pulling up the left side of your jacket so I can see what's making that bulge on your hip?"

Orland's features hardened as he complied, exposing a Starr double-action .44. "Now how did that get there?" he said and, using one hand, undid his buckle so the holstered weapon would succumb to the pull of gravity.

Fargo relaxed a smidgen, pleased by the turn of events. He had them disarmed. Now all he had to do was get the women out of there and safely back into Abilene. "All right," he said, about to issue orders, when there was movement on the gully floor and he saw a sight that made him realize all his effort might have been for nothing.

The young hothead, Clancy, his mouth all bloody, had revived enough to twist and clutch at his pearl-handled Colt.

4

This time both Orland and Bell were looking the other way, and none of the other gunmen had noticed either because, to a man, they were balefully gazing at Fargo. The only one who could stop Clancy was Fargo himself. With the thought came action, and as Clancy's fingers closed on those pearl grips, Fargo shifted, took a hasty bead, and touched the front trigger. The Sharps boomed and bucked.

Clancy was tilting the revolver upward when the slug ripped through his forehead and blew out the back of his skull.

The other gunmen, not knowing who Fargo was shooting at, had instinctively recoiled at the blast, all except Bell who stood poised and still with his arms folded, as unruffled as if he were merely standing at a depot waiting for a train.

Fargo took all of this in as he lowered the Sharps in his left hand and streaked out the Colt with his right. So swiftly did he move that there was no time for Tom Orland to dive for the Starr .44 before the Colt was fixed on his midsection. Everyone heard the click of the hammer being thumbed back. "Anyone else care to take a chance?" he demanded.

Orland was staring at the spreading pool of blood that framed Clancy's tousled hair. "Relax, mister," he said harshly. "You've made believers out of us." He looked up. "I suppose you gave Mullins the same treatment?"

"Mullins?" Fargo repeated, then understood. "Oh, him. Someone should give your men lessons in how to open doors quietly."

"He's dead?" Orland asked, and when Fargo nodded, he frowned. "That's a pity. He was a good man. I sent him to make sure you stayed put while I finished my business in Abilene. You'd already butted your nose in once with Bell, and I didn't want you causing me more aggravation. No one was supposed to get killed."

"You could have fooled me." Fargo hefted the Colt. "Now I'll ask the questions. I'd like to know why you were all set to whip Miss Walker within an inch of her life."

"Ask her," Orland said. "I'll never tell."

"I'll have to ask her later. First there's some business to take care of." Fargo's eyes locked on Susan's. "Mount up and head for town. Take all the horses with you, and take all their guns along. Don't stop no matter what you might hear."

"What are you fixing to do?" the black-haired beauty wanted to know.

"Make it hard for these men to bother you again." Fargo nodded at the horses. "Now hurry up." He didn't want any of the other gunmen to grow impatient and make a try for their hardware. If he shot another one, the rest just might throw caution to the wind and all dive for their pistols at once. Already one or two had acquired an edgy look, and it wouldn't take much to drive them over the brink of self-control.

No words were spoken as the women picked up the gunbelts and hastened to the horses. They mounted with difficulty, most showing by their awkward attempts that they were unaccustomed to riding. Susan Walker and Danette were the only ones who swung right up. At length all of them were in the saddle, and with much shouting and flapping of limbs they rode out of the gully and into the night.

"I know you from somewhere," Bell abruptly said.

Fargo slowly stood. Now that the gang was disarmed, he tried relaxing again. He moved to the edge of the drop-off and said, "Maybe you do. I get around." His Colt wagged from right to left, encompassing them all. "You boys have been so courteous, I almost hate to impose on you again. But I've decided to take up a new hobby. Collecting boots."

"You son of a bitch!" a beefy man snapped.

"Now, now. Don't spoil everything, not if you want to part on friendly terms," Fargo said pleasantly. He jabbed the Colt at Orland. "Since you're the cock of the roost, you can go first. Strip them off and back up."

"You're making a mistake, mister," Orland said as he sat down. Taking hold of his right boot, he tugged and pulled until it popped off. "You'd better kill us now, or so help me God you won't live out the week."

"Boss! Don't be giving him any ideas!" begged another of the bunch.

"That's all right," Fargo said, smirking. "You miserable lowlifes are lucky. I'm not the kind to go around killing unarmed men." His smirk was transformed into a scowl. "But I'm serving notice here and now. If I catch any of you on my trail, or if I find you've been bothering those ladies again, then I won't be so charitable."

"Big words," scoffed Orland. "Are we supposed to quake in fear? Hell, mister, you're tough, but it'll take a tougher bastard than you to stop us from doing what we have to do." He snorted. "Coming across as so high and mighty! The way you talk, a person would think you were Cullen Baker or Kit Carson or maybe even the Trailsman."

One and all, other than Bell, they vented scornful chuckles and chortles.

Skye Fargo wanted to avoid further bloodshed if he possibly could. As Susan Walker had noted earlier in the day, in his countless treks across the untamed West he had acquired a reputation rivaled by few others, and sometimes it worked to his advantage. Particularly when he wanted to discourage would-be curly wolves from bothering him. So now, as the hardcases below enjoyed a hearty laugh at his expense, he fixed his flinty eyes on Orland and announced, "As a matter of fact, I am. The name is Fargo. Skye Fargo."

The laughter died as if extinguished by a puff of wind.

"I knew it," Bell growled.

"Jesus!" declared another. "No one said anything about havin' to tangle with the likes of you!"

"Oh, Lord," said a third. "You can count me out of this from here on out."

"I want those boots off," Fargo commanded, "and I wouldn't keep me waiting if I was you." He wagged the Colt for emphasis, and this time not a single protest was voiced. Boots thudded to the ground just as fast as the wearers could strip them off. In three shakes of a lamb's tail every member of Orland's band was in their stocking feet, some with their toes protruding from large holes.

"I'm glad the wind isn't blowing from you to me," Fargo remarked, then indicated the south end of the gully. "Now I want all of you to start walking."

"I'll remember this," Orland rumbled.

"You do that," Fargo said. He stayed abreast of them as they moved out onto the prairie, his Colt fixed on their leader the entire time. They halted once they were in the open, and Bell spoke.

"What now, Trailsman? As if I can't guess."

"I hear tell that a little exercise does wonders for the constitution," Fargo answered. "And since it's such a fine night for a walk, you boys can start heading west. Do yourselves a favor and don't stop until you reach Pike's Peak."

Obediently, most of them began hiking off.

"But before you go," Fargo went on, "there's unfinished business to take care of."

They halted, a few sharing nervous glances, as Fargo leveled the Colt and walked up to Tom Orland. "Did you really think you'd get off this easy?"

"You'd better think twice," Orland said. "You're in the wrong here. And I tried to give you a warning not to meddle there by the eating house."

"Figured that was you," Fargo said flatly, and struck, his right arm a blur as he slammed the barrel of his Colt into Orland's temple. The man's legs sagged and he slumped to his knees. None of the others made any move to intervene as Fargo landed two more blows in swift succession and Orland toppled to the grass, blood trickling from his split forehead. "And this," Fargo said, "is for sending Mullins after me." Drawing back his right leg, he kicked with all his might, planting the tip of his boot in Orland's ribs. There was a distinct crack.

"Oh, God!" whispered one of the gunmen.

"Get this son of a bitch out of my sight," Fargo said, backing up so they wouldn't be able to jump him.

Bell motioned, and several of the men stepped forward to cart Orland off. The tall man lingered. He offered a begrudging smile and touched a finger to the tip of his hat. "I've got to hand it to you, Trailsman. You're everything they say you are." He paused. "But you're in the wrong this time. Orland has a legitimate interest in those women. If you knew why you were risking your life, you'd laugh yourself silly."

Fargo shrugged. "Maybe I am making a mistake. If so, it won't be the first time. And legitimate interest or not, Orland doesn't have the right to take a bullwhip to Susan Walker."

"She's not what she seems," Bell said. "None of them are. You're in the wrong here. And after what you just did to Tom, he won't rest until he evens the score."

"Be smart, Bell. Convince him to forget about those ladies."

"I couldn't if I tried. They're his, Fargo, to do with as he damn well pleases. Ask them. Make them tell you the reason behind all of this. Then see if you still want to meddle."

Troubled, Fargo watched the tall man walk off. Both Orland and Bell were so smug, so sure Orland was in the right, that Fargo couldn't help but wonder if there was a kernel of truth to Orland's claim. For all he knew, Orland might be Susan's husband and the two had had a falling out. Maybe she was using her maiden name or had changed it. Stranger things had happened.

Fargo still couldn't get over how friendly Orland's bunch and the women had been acting when he first saw them together, and it was that and that alone which had stayed his hand and stopped him from gunning Orland down instead of merely giving the dandy a taste of his own medicine.

But as Fargo reentered the gully he entertained doubts. If Orland was on the level, why all the secrecy? Why had Orland lain in wait in Abilene for the women to show, then hid out so the women wouldn't know he was there? The whole affair was one gigantic riddle, and Fargo didn't have a hint as to the solution.

Shutting the mystery from his mind, Fargo picked up one of the boots and hurled it far over the east side of the gully into the grass. One by one he did the same with each and every boot, and he grinned as he thought of how sore Orland's men would be when they came back and discovered the footwear gone.

A gusty breeze hit Fargo as he headed across the plain to the spot where he had left the Ovaro. He remembered to feed a new cartridge into the Sharps. As he was levering the trigger guard down, an invisible bee buzzed past his head at the very instant he heard the crack of a gun.

Fargo dived, going prone with the Sharps held in front of him. Mentally cursing himself for being a fool and not checking the gunmen to see if any of them had been carrying hide-outs, he snaked a dozen yards to the left, then halted.

The night was deathly still again, the prairie tranquil except for the rustling of the grass.

For a while Fargo waited to learn if they would try to close in on him, but nothing happened. Impatient to reach the Ovaro and get back to town to check on the women, he rose into a crouch and glided southward once again. The moon was bright enough for him to see fairly well for a distance of fifteen yards; beyond that point everything was shrouded in murk.

Suddenly another gunshot cracked. A slug snipped at grass in front of Fargo. Taking a long stride, he leaped and flattened himself on the ground, his heart thumping in his chest. That one, he reflected, had been altogether too close. Whoever was shooting must have the eyes of a cat!

Uneventful minutes dragged by as Fargo scanned the plain constantly for a trace of the gunman. Eventually, he hoped, the man would show himself or otherwise give his presence away, so he was perfectly content to wait. That is, he was until it occurred to him that Orland's gang might swing around him and head for Abilene and in doing so, stumble on the pinto. If that happened he'd be stranded afoot and whoever took his horse could go fetch others.

Discarding caution, Fargo eased up, his back bent low, and sprinted toward his stallion. He hadn't gone five yards when the flash of a shot flared in the darkness and a bullet tore through the space he had just occupied. Shifting, Fargo answered with the Sharps, aiming at the spot where he'd just seen the flash, and as he did, another gunman joined the fight, firing at Fargo's own flash. He felt a tug at his shoulder and dropped down.

There were two men with guns! Fargo realized, and they had set him up as neatly as if he was a dumb greenhorn. He touched his shoulder and found the buckskin intact, but several of the whangs had been sheared off. Another fraction of an inch and the bullet would have drawn blood.

Fargo turned and scooted to the east, certain the pair would now be trying to converge on him from opposite directions. He planned to lead them away from the vicinity of the Ovaro and double back later on. Zigzagging, he traveled fifteen yards, then halted to search and listen.

To the north a black shadow moved against the slightly lighter backdrop of the night.

This time Fargo relied on the Colt, palming the six-shooter and firing twice. The shadow disappeared, but he had no way of telling if he had scored or missed. Rotating, he continued eastward for another ten yards, then cut to the south.

More minutes elapsed. Fargo's nerves were on the raw edge as he surveyed the waving grass in front of him. He was perhaps thirty yards from where he had left the pinto when the drumming of hoofs told him he was too late.

"Damn!" Fargo fumed, and stood, heedless of the risk. He ran to intercept the rider and abruptly saw that the man was accidentally coming straight toward him. Instantly he ducked down, holstered the Colt, and reversed his grip on the rifle.

The gunman was lashing the Ovaro with the reins and flapping his legs as if he were trying to lay an egg. He had his eyes glued on the distant lights of Abilene, and so intent was he on getting out of there, he failed to pay much attention to the ground in front of him.

Fargo had to shift a few feet so as not to be ridden down. He expected the rider to spot him and swerve aside, but the man didn't. As the stallion galloped closer, he firmed his hold on the cool metal barrel, tensed his shoulders, and balanced on the balls of his feet. Then, as the stallion swept even with his hiding place, he surged upright and swung the Sharps like a club.

Caught on the head, the gunman flew from the saddle and crashed to the earth in a disjointed heap.

The Ovaro hardly slowed, but at a low whistle from Fargo the big horse dug in its hoofs and slid to a stop. Fargo raced to catch up, while to the north and west pistols blasted. He was going all out when he came up behind the pinto and vaulted into the air. His out-flung legs cleared the stallion's hindquarters and he alighted behind his bedroll. A shove carried him over the bedroll and into the saddle, where he leaned down to grasp the reins even as his spurs goaded the Ovaro into a gallop again.

To the north, the gunman had emptied his cylinder and the firing had ceased, but two more shots echoed from the west.

Fargo was hunched low over the stallion's neck. Neither shot came close, and in seconds they were out of effective range. He shoved the Sharps into the boot, pulled his hat down tight so the wind wouldn't yank it off, and altered his course slightly to make a beeline for the town.

A grin creased Fargo's mouth. He had thwarted Orland once more, and the dandy was bound to be more furious then ever. Once he reached Abilene, he intended to corner Susan Walker and learn exactly what was going on. This time he wouldn't let her put him off.

Suddenly Fargo heard a grunt behind him and to his left. He twisted, his right hand falling to his Colt, but his fingers had barely touched the butt when a pair of brawny arms encircled him around the middle and he was propelled from the saddle as if he'd been plowed into by a battering ram. His shoulder bore the brunt of the impact, lancing pain through his arm and side. Before he could scramble to his feet, a heavy fist gouged into his stomach, another brushed his chin.

Fargo got a hand on the ground for support, and turned. One of Orland's gang stood over him, poised to deliver a haymaker. Fargo's right boot kicked out, connecting with the gunman's knee. The man cried out, then staggered backward, allowing Fargo the breathing space needed to stand. He went for his Colt but his fingers closed on empty air and he realized the six-shooter had fallen loose when he'd been unhorsed.

Growling like a feral beast, the gunman attacked. He was nowhere near as skilled as Bell had been. His swings were wild, and he neglected to set himself.

Still, Fargo knew he might well lose if he miscalculated. His forearm blocked a blow aimed at his face. In retaliation he drove his right fist into the man's stomach, and when the gunman snapped forward, Fargo gave him a knee in the nose. Something crunched and the man let out a strangled howl and sagged to the grass. Fargo put him out of his misery with a kick to the jawbone.

Deceptive tranquility reclaimed the prairie. Ten yards away stood the Ovaro, waiting, its tail flicking. Fargo rubbed his sore shoulder and cast about for the lost Colt. The high grass hindered him, and he didn't know if the revolver had slipped straight to the ground or been sent sailing. He searched at the spot where he believed the stallion had been when the hardcase jumped him, but although he got down on his hands and knees and felt around in the flattened grass, he failed to find it.

Fargo was annoyed by this new delay in reaching Abilene. He worried that Orland might have left a man in town, and if the women came riding in they'd find themselves held at gunpoint once again. The unconscious hardcase groaned, and Fargo stared at him, speculating on how the man had happened to be at that particular spot just as Fargo came by. He concluded that Orland, or more likely Bell, must have sent the fastest runner in the bunch toward town the moment the gang walked out of his sight. He'd underestimated them and mustn't make the mistake again.

Since the Colt was nowhere in the vicinity of where he'd been knocked off the pinto, Fargo broadened his hunt, moving in ever-widening circles. He mentally crossed his fingers that the moonlight would glint off the metal and help him locate the six-gun, but the ground was enveloped in gloomy shadow.

More precious time ticked slowly by. Fargo began to glance westward now and then to make certain Bell and the rest weren't approaching. They would, eventually, if they were taking the straightest course to town.

His vexation mounting, Fargo halted twenty feet from where he had tussled with the gunman. The Colt couldn't possibly have flown that far. He carefully worked his way back, going over every square inch, yet the pistol remained lost. The gunman groaned again and stirred; he might soon revive. Fargo had to find his gun and make tracks.

Pausing, Fargo placed his hands on his hips and scoured the grass for a section he might have missed. Low voices abruptly carried to his ears, and whirling, he spied a cluster of obscure forms off to the west. It was Orland's men, and they might spot him at any second!

Doubling over, Fargo quickened the pace of his search, his hands constantly roving, probing, feeling. The voices grew steadily louder. Soon the words were audible.

"—just a damned scratch, so quit your whining! We'll get you patched up once we're in town."

That had been Bell.

"You wouldn't say it was a scratch if it'd been you he shot. I'm bleedin' to death, I tell you," complained the man Fargo had winged.

"If you don't shut your mouth, bleeding to death will be the least of your worries," Bell declared.

Fargo still hadn't found his Colt. He was about ready to

47

chalk it up as hopelessly lost and get to the stallion. A shout confirmed he should.

"Hey! Look there! Is that a horse?"

Lingering was out of the question. Fargo sped toward his pinto, but on his second stride his left foot bumped something hard and, looking down, he found his six-shooter at last. As he bent over to pick it up, he heard a pistol bark, then another. Slugs whipped past on either side. Pivoting, he saw the gunmen coming on fast.

Fargo fired once to slow them and every last man dropped. He pumped his legs, weaving to present less of a target, and reached the stallion just as the gunmen opened up again, their pistols cracking in a steady cadence. The Ovaro began to run. Fargo had to throw out his hands and seize hold of the saddle horn, and he was half-dragged, half-carried for a dozen feet before he could coil his legs and swing smoothly up into the saddle.

The shots and yells dwindled. Once again Fargo had barely escaped with his hide intact. He jammed the Colt into his holster and worked the reins, bringing the pinto to a full gallop. They raced across the moonlit plain.

Presently Fargo could see the individual buildings in Abilene. There were ten or more people gathered outside of the saloon, all staring westward. Among them he spotted Adeline, the bartender, and Rice. He slowed, trotted along the street, and reined up when he came close to them.

"What's all the shooting about, stranger?" someone demanded.

"Yeah. What in tarnation were you doin' out there, mister?" asked another.

Fargo ignored them and smiled at Adeline. "I didn't have time to say so long earlier, so I'm doing it now."

"You're leaving for good?" she responded sadly.

"Afraid so. I have to escort five pilgrims and their wagons all the way to the Rockies."

"You mean those ladies?" Adeline asked in surprise.

"Yep."

"Then you'd best shake a leg."

"Why?"

Grinning, Adeline turned and pointed down the street at the livery.

The Conestogas were gone.

5

A crimson streak tinged the distant eastern horizon when Skye Fargo opened his eyes and yawned. Beside him, his tiny fire had long since dwindled to charred ashes. Close by, securely tethered to a picket pin firmly imbedded in the ground, grazed the stallion.

Fargo had decided to sleep out on the plain rather than remain in Abilene and risk another confrontation with Orland's men. He'd bought the few supplies he needed at the general store and departed just as Bell and the others straggled into town. Adeline had stood waving near the back door of the saloon, bathed in the soft light from within, long after he was out of her sight.

Sitting up, he threw off his blanket and stood. For as far as he could see in all directions rippled an ocean of grass. Abilene lay several miles to the east. A quarter of a mile to the north was the trail westward, and Susan Walker and her friends should be somewhere along it. He expected to overtake them well before noon, even if they had traveled all night.

A hot cup of coffee and breakfast would have to wait. Fargo expected Orland to give chase at dawn. If he wanted to reach the women first, he must head out immediately.

It took less than five minutes to roll the blankets and throw his saddle on the Ovaro. The picket pin went back in his saddle bags. Then, with the wind in his hair, he galloped to the rutted trail and turned westward.

Although at first glance the prairie seemed to be a semiarid wasteland, it abounded with wildlife. Antelope were numerous, and those nearest the trail bounded off at incredible speeds when the horseman appeared. Deer were plentiful, too, both bucks and does. Huge prairie-dog towns dotted the grassland, and when sentries spied the speeding stallion they would voice their shrill alarms and the entire population, whether in the hundreds or the thousands, would dive for cover. Hawks soared on high, while smaller birds winged past on their way to far-off trees.

Fargo rode loosely, an extension of his horse, the fringe on his buckskins swaying with the motion of the Ovaro. He was glad to be out among the wide-open spaces again, to be back in the wild land he loved so much. Towns and cities were all right for a while, for a day or a week of drinking and gambling and womanizing. But in due course the entertainment always staled, and Fargo was ready to venture into the untamed regions of the frontier again.

Fresh wagon tracks confirmed Fargo was right about the women heading west. He didn't blame them for not sticking around. They were scared Orland would catch them, and they'd probably press on until they were too exhausted to go any farther.

Several times Fargo spooked rabbits, and he was tempted to drop one on the fly to save for a later meal. But he resisted the impulse since he had no idea how close behind him Orland's gang might be, and he didn't want them to hear the shot. They'd probably suspect he was the one ahead of them and ride hard to catch him.

The unending expanse of grassland seldom changed. Isolated stands of trees intermittently appeared, and once, to the south, a string of cottonwoods indicated the location of a creek.

At midmorning Fargo came to where the women had briefly stopped during the middle of the night to rest their mules. They had been pushing their teams and made excellent progress, yet in doing so they were wearing the mules out quickly. Once they finally stopped, they'd have to rest a full day to give their teams time to recuperate.

An hour shy of noon, Fargo spied twin white mounds at the limits of his vision, moving mounds that shortly resolved themselves into the outlines of the canvas-topped Conestogas. He smiled and goaded the stallion to move a bit faster.

Several hundred yards had yet to be covered when Fargo saw a small cloud of smoke billow from the rear of the last wagon and heard the retort of a rifle. Slowing, he removed his hat and waved it overhead while shouting, "Hold your fire! I'm on your side!"

Both wagons drew to a stop. All five women appeared,

three holding rifles, the rest pistols. They formed a line behind the last wagon and waited for him.

"Was that any way to greet a friend?" Fargo asked as he drew rein. "I went through a hell of a lot last night for you knotheads. The least you could do is hold off trying to kill me until you hear what I want."

Danette sheepishly cradled the rifle she held in the crook of a slender elbow and responded, "Sorry. That was me who fired. I just happened to glance up and saw someone coming. I shot without taking time to see who it was."

Susan Walker stepped near and rested her hand on Fargo's arm. "Please accept our apology. We do owe you a debt of gratitude for the service you rendered last night. That was very noble of you."

"Noble, hell. I just don't like to see folks pushed around." Fargo removed his hat and wiped his perspiring forehead with the back of his sleeve. "If your mules are half as hot as I am, you'd better stop soon or they're liable to keel over."

"We were hoping to reach water first," Susan said. "We left Abilene in such a hurry that we forgot to fill our water keg and our spare water skins."

Fargo squinted up at the blazing sun, then donned his hat. "The nearest watering hole is ten miles west of here. If we're lucky we'll reach it before nightfall. Climb back in those wagons and let's get going."

Susan's hand squeezed his arm lightly. "Does this mean you've changed your mind and you're willing to guide us to Mountain City?"

"I didn't come all this way just to pass the time of day," Fargo replied, grinning. Some of the women cried out in delight, and he swore he saw moisture rim Susan's striking eyes.

"You have no idea how happy this makes us," she said softly, her hand lingering.

Was there a hint of a suggestion in the tone she used, in the pressure of her fingers? Fargo wondered, his eyes devouring the ripe contours of her full figure. She stepped back, her cheeks reddening slightly, and coughed.

"All right, ladies. We have the answer to our prayers. Now let's prove to ourselves and to those who are waiting for us that we deserve this chance. Back in the wagons. We have a water hole to make by dark."

They did it, too, by pushing the mules to the limits of their endurance. Fargo was considerably impressed by the skill the women displayed in handling the teams and the big wagons; they did about as good a job as the average mule skinner. For his part, he kept busy scouting ahead for Indian signs, and checking to the rear at least once an hour for signs of Tom Orland. Neither danger had presented itself by the time the flaming sun hung on the flat rim of the earth, and the Conestogas rolled to a lumbering stop beside the water hole.

"We did it!" Danette cried gleefully.

On their own, the five women expertly stripped the harness off the mules, let the animals drink their fill, and led them off to graze. Audris stood watch, a rifle in hand, while Catherine got a fire going and Danette and Rita unloaded the victuals for their supper.

Fargo was pleasantly surprised to find he had nothing to do but take care of the Ovaro. He remarked as much when Susan strolled over, a pretty red shawl draped over her slim shoulders.

"We've had plenty of practice. Sometimes it feels like we've been on the trail forever." Susan arched her back and stretched, her bosom swelling against her dress. "I swear that none of us have ever worked so hard in our entire lives. But it will all be worth it once we reach Mountain City." She paused. "At least I hope it will."

"Is it prying to ask what's waiting for you there?" Fargo inquired casually.

Susan glanced at him, furrow lines molding her forehead. "I don't know," she said hesitantly, and seemed to be grappling with a decision. "What can it hurt?" she said after a bit. "You might as well know now and save us all embarrassment later on. We have husbands waiting for us."

"You're all married?"

"No, but we will be once we get there. Five of the sweetest, kindest men west of the Mississippi are waiting anxiously for our arrival, and once we reach them there's going to be a wedding the likes of which the Rocky Mountains haven't seen since the dawn of time." Her features radiated sheer bliss at the heartwarming picture she painted. "You'll see. You'll be welcome to stick around and take part in the festivities."

"I'll keep it in mind," Fargo said, disguising his puzzled

state. He'd never heard of five women all being hitched at the same time. And if the husbands-to-be were all that she made out, then why weren't the men there now escorting their women across the perilous prairie instead of cooling their heels in Mountain City?

Susan went off to lend a hand cooking. Presently the mouth-watering odor of the boiling food brought Fargo over to the fire where a stew bubbled in a large black pot suspended on a tripod over the dancing flames. "That sure smells good," he complimented them.

"You really think so?" Rita responded. "We've been practicing real hard. Why, before this all began, there wasn't one of us except maybe Sue here who could boil water without burning the pan."

"Is that a fact?" Fargo said, his puzzlement growing. What sort of lives had these women been leading that they hadn't learned to cook? It was one of the first things young girls learned from their mothers, and virtually every woman on the frontier rightfully prided herself on this ability. There were exceptions, but they were city-bred women who ate at fancy restaurants most of the time or had servants who did the cooking for them.

Sue had turned at Rita's comment. "Dear, I'm sure Mr. Fargo doesn't care to hear all about our shortcomings." Her voice lowered to stress her next statement. "Our private lives are really no one's business but our own. Isn't that right?"

"Yes," Rita said meekly. "Sorry, Sue. But it's so darn hard."

"Keep practicing."

"Practicing what?" Fargo interjected.

"Why, how to be the very best wives and women we can possibly be," Susan answered. "We want our husbands to be pleased with us."

"I doubt you have much to worry about," Fargo said, surveying the five of them with the appreciative eye of a man who had known far more than his share of women. "You're about five of the loveliest ladies I've ever come across, and it'd be my guess that the men waiting for you all feel the same way."

"But they've never seen us before," Danette blurted, and stiffened when the other women spun on her.

"Oh?" was all Fargo could think of to say. Surprise was

piling on top of surprise. Who'd ever heard of women venturing across a sizeable chunk of Indian territory—and putting their lives at risk from relentless elements and wild beasts—in order to marry men they'd never even met? It was downright strange.

"We have written to one another," Susan said quickly. "Many, many times. I'd say between the five of us we've shared several hundred letters with our intendeds."

"That's nice," Fargo said lamely, although in truth he was thinking that he had never heard of such a harebrained proposition in all his life.

"We met them through *The Heart and Hand*," Susan explained.

And suddenly Fargo understood. *The Heart and Hand* was one of the most popular magazines in the West. Put out by a matrimonial bureau, it specialized in listing the names, addresses, and short personal sketches of lovelorn women eager to meet the men of their dreams. Most were widows who had no other way of meeting men, or women whose physical charms weren't quite the equal of their writing skill. And hardly any, from what Fargo had heard, were as young and attractive as the five women he was with.

"You must think this quite silly of us," Susan said, "but you wouldn't if you understood fully." She brushed at her hair and the firelight played on her beautiful face. "Looks aren't everything in life. Sometimes a pretty woman has a harder time finding the right man than other women might because a lot of men are so afraid to talk to her that they shy away. Haven't you ever been to a social and seen the prettiest girl there standing by herself in a corner?"

"Yes," Fargo admitted.

"That's why." Susan indicated her companions. "We've all had a similar problem, and we solved it by advertising in *The Heart and Hand*. Each of us received dozens of replies, and it took us months to weed out the ones that didn't sound promising. Finally we narrowed our choices down to the five men in Mountain City."

Fargo thoughtfully scratched his chin. What were the odds of five women who knew each other all receiving love letters from five men who happened to live in the same place? Something didn't quite ring true here.

As if Susan Walker could read his mind, she went on. "They're all miners, you see, and they answered our ads as a lark. They never really intended to get married. They just wanted someone to share their thoughts with."

That sounded true enough. Fargo knew of several men who had responded to one of the listings as a joke and wound up marrying women whose endowments didn't quite match up to their expectations. The five in Mountain City were in for quite a pleasant shock.

"Now," Susan said, rubbing her palms together, "enough about us. Supper is ready, so why don't we eat?"

The meal was conducted, for the most part, in silence. Fargo noticed that every last woman appeared to be upset but was trying not to show it. He couldn't figure out why, but he did know they were hiding something. What could it be?

Young Catherine and Rita washed the tin plates and spoons. Danette set up a rope corral using the wagons as anchors at each end, and Susan and Audris brought the mules into the makeshift enclosure for the night.

Fargo sat by the warm fire and pondered on how he had been doing it wrong all these years. He'd hired out as guide to wagon trains before and the job had been nothing like this. Ordinarily he'd be kept busy from dawn, working his backside off to ensure that everything ran smoothly. But not so with these women. They were as independent as most men and competent to boot. He could sit around taking it easy while they did the work. From here on out, he mentally noted with a grin, he should only guide wagon trains of women.

Susan came over. "I thought I would let you know there's no need for you to stay up keeping watch tonight. We have a schedule worked out, and we each take a turn standing guard. So you can get a good night's sleep."

"Can I get breakfast in bed in the morning?" Fargo joked.

Her laugh was delightful. "Afraid not. We'll have to draw the line somewhere. All you need worry about is reaching the Rocky Mountains safely. You'll get the money I promised you when we do."

"I'm not doing this for the money," Fargo told her.

"Oh," Susan said. Then, on seeing the hungry look in his piercing eyes, she said again, only softly, "Oh! But I thought we made it clear earlier? We're all betrothed. And proper ladies don't do such things."

"A man can admire a work of art without having to own it, can't he?" Fargo responded. "And don't fret. I'm not about to jump you in your sleep. However, if you should jump me, then it's a different story."

"None of us would do that," Susan said, and chuckled. But it sounded false, as if she didn't quite believe her own words. She added good-naturedly, "I do believe there's a little streak of the lecher in you, Mr. Fargo."

"No," Fargo corrected her. "I don't go lusting after every woman I see. But I've never had to beg, neither."

This time her cheeks were more scarlet than before. She excused herself and hurried to her wagon, her shawl pulled up around her chin even though the air was not yet all that cool.

All of the women were retiring except for Rita, who was standing watch. Fargo unrolled his bedroll and reclined on his back, his head resting in his hands. Around him milled the mules. He could hear muted conversations in both wagons and wondered if he was the topic. At length, as the flames steadily dwindled beside him, his eyelids drooped and he sank into dreamland . . . only to be awakened by the press of a hand over his mouth.

Fargo's eyes shot open and his right hand streaked for his Colt, but a whispering female voice in his ear showed there was no danger.

"Don't have a calf, Trailsman. I don't bite."

The hand was lifted. Since the fire had long since gone out and there was no moon this night, a veil of darkness lay thick on the land. Fargo could make out the outline of the woman beside him but her features were a black slate. "Rita?"

"No, silly. Catherine."

The heady fragrance of her perfume struck Fargo like a physical blow, and suddenly he realized she had a hand lying on his inner thigh. Any vestige of sleep vanished. He was fully awake and feeling faint stirrings in his loins. He was also confused. This was the same woman who had seemed so young and had been so terrified when Susan had berated her for her earlier behavior toward Fargo. "What the hell are you up to?" he growled.

"Shhhhh! Not so loud! We don't want to wake up the others."

"We don't?"

"I just wanted to have a little chat with you."

"At this time of night? Aren't you on guard duty?"

"Everything is quiet except for the damn coyotes." Catherine lowered herself until her body brushed his, then said as if mocking him, "But if you'd rather I let you get back to sleep, say the word."

"I don't like playing games," Fargo said.

"Neither do I, big man."

"Prove it," Fargo said, and swept his left hand up to her breasts. She tensed at the contact, then gasped as he squeezed hard. Her mouth, soft and moist and tantalizing, came down on his and her silken tongue darted out, caressing his tongue. At the same time her hands began rubbing his legs, warming them by the friction and producing a marked tingling in his loins.

Fargo wasn't prepared for the intensity of Catherine's physical hunger. She seemed to be trying to suck his mouth up into hers, and her breaths came in great puffs like those of an idling train. Her body molded to his, her hips grinding her nether mound into his manhood. He had the impression she was starved for sex, an impression confirmed when she finally broke for air.

"It's been so long! So very long!"

Fargo had been massaging her breasts the whole time. Now she reached up and pressed her hands down on top of his so that he mashed her globes harder. A cooing sound fluttered from her throat. She closed her eyes, quivered, and licked her lips.

"Damn! You have no idea how this makes me feel."

"I have a fair notion," Fargo responded. He was amazed at the amount of heat her body generated from between her legs, so much that he felt it through both her clothes and his. His right hand drifted down across her flat stomach to the junction of her thighs and he cupped her with the palm of his hand.

"Uhhhnnnn," Catherine husked, her face drooping onto his shoulder. "I'm so glad you changed your mind about coming."

Fargo's left hand caressed her thighs. She parted them to grant him easier access, and he slipped the hand between her legs and stroked leisurely. Her breath was hot in his ear, her fingers digging into his arms.

Just then, from within the nearest wagon, came a soft thud, as if someone within had knocked over something.

Catherine's head shot up and she cast an apprehensive glance at the canvas top. "Oh, no!" she whispered. "It's her! I just know it!" She abruptly disentangled herself and pushed to her feet. "Say nothing," she advised him as she bent over to retrieve her rifle. Then she dashed into the darkness.

Fargo barely had time to collect his wits and wonder what in the hell was going on when a figure stepped down from the wagon and came hastily toward him. He recognized the hip-length, flowing hair of Susan Walker. She was bundled in a heavy robe pulled discreetly up to her chin. He couldn't say what prompted him to close his eyes and pretend to be sound asleep, but he did, and a moment later heard her address him quietly.

"Fargo? Are you awake?"

Hoping he put the right amount of feigned drowsiness into his voice, Fargo mumbled, "What? What is it?" Blinking, he slowly lifted his head and looked around until his gaze fastened on her. "Something wrong?"

"I thought I heard voices out here."

"You must have imagined it," Fargo said, and rubbed his eyes as one does when first awakened from deep sleep.

"I could almost swear I did," Susan insisted suspiciously, glancing around the camp. "One of them was yours."

"Sometimes I talk a little in my sleep. Most folks do," Fargo said, and laid his head down again. He saw Catherine stroll around the end of the other wagon and come toward them.

"Sue? What in the world are you doing up? I'm not due to be relieved for two more hours yet."

"Were you just talking with Fargo?" Susan demanded.

"Hell, no. Whatever gives you that idea? I've been standing over there listening to the howling of those adorable coyotes."

"But I know I heard voices."

"You might have heard this big clown," Catherine said, jerking a thumb at Fargo. "A while ago I heard him mumbling to himself. He snores loud, too."

Susan scrutinized first Fargo, then Catherine. Apparently she made up her mind that they were telling the truth, because she nodded and said, "All right. Sorry to have disturbed you." She faced Catherine. "You can go back to keeping watch." Then she waited until the younger woman had walked off before she turned to leave herself.

"Hold on," Fargo said. "What difference would it make if she had been talking to me?"

Halting, Susan stared at him, her features impossible to interpret in the darkness. "Perhaps none. Perhaps all the difference in the world." She adjusted her robe tighter around her waist. "As I told you before, you have quite a reputation. And I don't mean your reputation for mayhem. I mean your reputation with the ladies. Since the others saw fit to pick me to be our leader on our journey to the Rockies, it's my responsibility to make certain that you don't live up to your reputation while you're with us. Do I make myself clear?"

"As a bell," Fargo responded.

"Excellent. From here on out, try to keep your nightly mutterings down to a whisper," Susan stated. Back stiff, shoulders straight, she marched to her wagon and climbed in.

"You can count on that," Fargo said to himself, rolling onto his back to alleviate the uncomfortable tightness caused by his hard manhood straining against his pants. His only other comment, uttered right before he drifted off again, was a single word: "Women!"

6

Skye Fargo was embarrassed to be the last one up the next morning. Normally he awakened at first light, so he was at a loss to explain why he slept in so late and had to be roused by a foot prodding his shoulder.

"Rise and shine, Mr. Fargo. A new day awaits."

Sitting bolt upright, Fargo was amazed to see that all the women were up, the fire had been rekindled, and three of the ladies were hitching the mules to the wagons. The upper third of the sun had already peeked above the horizon, lending the gently waving prairie grass a shimmering golden glow.

"You surprise me," Susan Walker commented. "I always thought that you big, rugged frontier sorts were up before the roosters, but that must be another of those tall tales they put in those cheap books the children are forever reading."

"Wake up in a sour mood this morning, did we?" Fargo countered gruffly as he rose.

"Not at all," Susan replied, smiling. "Ever since we left St. Louis, I've been raring to go each morning. When a person is starting their life over, every day is new and indescribably precious."

"If you say so," Fargo grumbled, stepping to the coffee pot. A tin cup had been placed out for him and he filled it to the brim, then hunkered down and sipped gingerly. The coffee burned a path from his mouth to his stomach, jolting his sluggish senses. He saw Catherine helping out with the mules but she studiously ignored him.

"We've been talking," Susan said, coming over. "And we're all extremely worried about Orland. He'll probably catch up with us today, won't he?"

"If he's after you."

"He is. Have no doubt about that. Tom won't rest until he's dragged us back to St. Louis whether we want to go or not. If need be, he'll follow us all the way to the mountains."

"Does he know you're headed for Mountain City?"

"No. Why?"

"If he does, he might take it into his head to swing on around you and wait for you there. That's what he did in Abilene, isn't it?"

"Yes," Susan admitted, "but I can't see him letting us get that far. Every mile we travel makes the return journey that much longer." She turned eastward. "I know him, Fargo, as well as I do myself. After our escape, he'll be twice as determined to teach us a lesson. He's probably in the saddle right this minute."

"Then we'd better do the same," Fargo suggested, standing. "You head out while I check our back trail. As many men as he's got, I should spot their dust a ways off and have time to set up a proper welcome."

"You're a man after my own heart," Susan said, grinning. Forgetting herself, she raised her hand to caress his cheek. For a moment she was totally at ease and there was no mistaking the affection she displayed for him. But the moment passed. She caught herself and jerked her arm down as if she had touched a porcupine.

"Sorry," Sue mumbled.

"Don't be," Fargo said. He glimpsed Danette off to one side. She had noticed and was smiling slyly as if at an inner joke. Why? In several large gulps he polished off the coffee and handed the cup to Susan. "Expect to see me before noon. Keep your eyes peeled, and if you need me fire three shots in the air every so often until I show up."

"Take care of yourself, Skye."

Nodding, Fargo hurriedly assembled his bedroll, threw his saddle over his shoulder, and walked to the Ovaro. As he set down the bedroll so he could throw his saddle blanket on the stallion, he realized that had been the first time she had called him by his first name.

The women were taking their seats in the Conestogas when Fargo gave a wave and rode to the east. He had no plan beyond confirming whether Orland was indeed after them and somehow stopping the dandy from bothering the women ever again. In that respect the Sharps might be all he needed. No other rifle made could match its range and accuracy. All he had to do was find a convenient spot and pick off one or two of Orland's men from half a mile away. That should convince the rest to leave the women be.

Since Fargo had neglected to eat any breakfast, he pulled several pieces of jerked venison from his saddlebags and munched on them as he rode. Once the wagons were out of sight he was all alone in the great vastness of the plains, seemingly the sole living creature within miles. Later on he saw the usual wildlife; prairie dogs, hawks, and a few antelope.

When the scorching sun was two hours high, Fargo reined up and got down to give the pinto a breather. As yet there was no trace of Orland, which Fargo was at a loss to explain. If the gang had left Abilene the morning after the incident at the gully, Fargo calculated they should be no more than five or six miles behind the wagons, if that. Yet he went eight miles and found no indication that anyone had used the trail since the Conestogas passed by.

For over twenty minutes Fargo waited and watched. No riders appeared; no dust showed. He toyed with the thought that Orland had given up, but his intuition told him otherwise. Perhaps, he reflected, Orland had some kind of clever strategy worked out, although Fargo had no idea what it might be.

After tightening the cinch, Fargo remounted and turned around. He'd been gone from the women long enough. Now that they were entering the fringe of Indian country, he didn't care to leave them for very long. Accordingly, he trotted over the same stretch of trail for the third time in twenty-four hours, and he swore he had every bump and clump of grass memorized.

Noon was still an hour and a half off when Fargo spied the wagons rolling ponderously westward. He caught up quickly, passing the rear wagon and moving alongside the first Conestoga.

Susan Walker promptly hauled on the reins and shouted at the mules, "Whoa! Whoa, there!" She gave the Trailsman an apprehensive look. "Did you see Orland?"

"No."

"I don't understand. Where could they be? Shouldn't they have caught up with us by this time?"

"The answer to your second question is yes," Fargo replied, resting his forearms on the saddle horn. "As for the first, your guess is as good as mine."

"I don't like this," Susan declared. "Orland can be as crafty as a fox when he wants to be. He must have concocted some sort of devious scheme."

"I was thinking the same thing."

"What do we do?"

"There's nothing we can do but keep on going and keep alert," Fargo said. "I'll ride ahead and find somewhere to make our noon stop. If you spot any dust behind you, do like I told you before and fire some shots."

Absently biting her lower lip, Susan nodded.

Fargo didn't blame her for being so upset. As leader, the safety of all five women was on her shoulders. And a mighty fine set of shoulders they were, as was the rest of her. He thought of how he'd like to share a bed with her sometime, then wryly shook his head and chuckled. He needed to heed his own advice and stay alert, not daydream about making love.

An isolated stand of aspen trees seemed the perfect place to let the Ovaro rest and await the wagons, so he tied the stallion to a low limb close to the trail and settled down with his back to a smooth trunk. A scan of the prairie had showed no life at all, as even the prairie dogs were seeking relief in their burrows from the oppressive heat of the midday sun. He pulled his hat brim low and relaxed.

In half an hour the squeak of metal-rimmed wheels brought Fargo to his feet. The mules were plodding methodically along, their tails flicking now and then, their bodies glistening with sweat. The women had made a wise choice in picking them. While not as hardy as oxen, mules were nearly as tireless and far less likely to suffer from overwork than horses. Mules were also faster than oxen, which was why settlers who didn't care to take forever to cross the plains and who had a little extra money to spend usually used them.

"No dust on our trail," Susan announced as she clambered down. "I'm beginning to think I was wrong and Tom has given up after all."

"He hasn't, lady," stated a gruff voice from within the trees.

Fargo whirled in surprise, his right hand closing on his Colt. But he stopped short of drawing, his eyes on the muzzle of a large-caliber buffalo gun pointed squarely at his midsection. Holding it was a grizzled, dirty man in shabby buckskins and an old beaver hat.

"I wouldn't, sonny," the man warned, and grinned wide, exposing a cavity where three of his top teeth had once been. "Old Sadie here will plumb blow a hole in you big enough to walk through." He hefted his rifle and snickered.

Another man stepped into view, a heftier, dirtier copy of the first, sporting a nasty scar on his left cheek. In addition to a rifle, he carried a Walker Colt jammed under his wide, brown leather belt. He also wore a perpetual scowl, and his beady black eyes glinted wickedly. "I reckon this is the easiest one hundred dollars we've ever earned, Eb."

"I'd say so, Justis," agreed his companion.

Fargo eased his hand off the Colt and held his arms out from his sides. He recognized these men for what they were: buffalo hunters. Scores like them were wandering the plains in pursuit of the huge herds, and if they continued to kill the great brutes as fast as they had been, in another twenty or thirty years there wouldn't be a single buffalo left. Which didn't bother them at all. The only thing they cared about was the money they received for the hides they sold.

"Who are you men?" Susan demanded. "What is the meaning of this outrage?"

"Ain't she a funny one!" Eb declared.

"And damn pretty, too," Justis said, devouring her with those beady eyes of his.

Just then Catherine, Rita, and Audris approached from the rear wagon. Only Rita was holding a rifle, and at the sight of the two grungy buffalo hunters she went to level it.

"Don't you, missy!" barked Justis, his own gun trained unerringly on Susan Walker. "Or sure as hell I'll rub out this she-critter with the fine dark hair. Throw your long-gun in the grass and be right quick about it."

Rita paused and glanced at Susan, who frowned and shook her head. In disgust, Rita tossed her rifle down.

The two hunters strode arrogantly forward, their faces shining with triumph, then halted a few yards away. They glanced at one another and cackled, and the older man, Eb, slapped his leg in delight.

"If this don't beat all! What do you figure these women are doin' all the way out here?"

"It don't matter," Justis said. "They ain't goin' another

foot until he comes, and he'd better have the hundred dollars he promised or we'll keep these gals for ourselves."

"Oh God!" Susan exclaimed as comprehension hit her like a physical blow. "Tom Orland hired you!"

"That he did, missy," Justis answered. "He's laid up back in Abilene with a busted rib and a bad head, thanks to this feller." His gun swiveled to cover the Trailsman. "A gent by the name of Bell came up to us in the saloon and asked us if we wanted to earn some spendin' money, and naturally we was interested. So he took us to meet Orland."

"Talk about riled!" Eb took up the story. "He's madder than a thorn-stuck panther at not bein' able to do any ridin' for a week or so, and he can't wait to get his paws on the one who whipped him." He smirked at Fargo.

"Please," Susan said. "We've done nothing to you. Let us go our way in peace. A hundred dollars can't mean so much to you that you'd risk breaking the law for it."

"Missy, when a man don't have a dollar to his name, a hundred dollars is all the money in the world," Justis informed her.

"Yeah," Eb added. "The buffalo huntin' has been right thin in this territory lately, and we need a stake before we move on. This here job is heaven-sent."

Fargo stayed silent. He knew he'd be wasting his breath if he tried to persuade the hunters to leave the women alone. Also, he was hoping the pair would become so wrapped up in their talk with Susan that he'd have a chance to go for his six-shooter. But fate dictated otherwise.

"Now before we all get acquainted, there's certain things we have to do," Eb said, advancing until the tip of his rifle barrel touched Fargo's chest. "First off, I want you to shed that hog-leg of yours, young feller. And do it real slow if you want to stay healthy."

As much as Fargo hated to comply, he had no choice. Using a single finger, he pulled the Colt out and let it slide off his finger into the grass at Eb's feet.

"Thank you," Eb said politely. Suddenly, without warning, he drove his rifle into Fargo's stomach, and when Fargo doubled over in pain, he slammed the stock against Fargo's skull.

"No!" Susan cried.

Pulses of agony punished Fargo's body as he collapsed. He braced himself on his hands and knees and inhaled raggedly, striving to fill his lungs again. Pinwheels of light dazzled him as he glanced up at the buffalo hunters.

"That's just a taste of what you'll get if you don't behave yourself," Eb declared. "Orland said he wanted you alive, but he also said we could do as we pleased if you showed any spunk." He tapped Fargo's nose with the cool metal barrel. "Savvy, mister?"

"Yes," Fargo rasped.

"I hope so, for your sake." Eb picked up the Colt and wedged it under his belt. His tongue jutting from the gap in his teeth, he turned toward the first wagon. "What are you still doin' up there, lady? Light off there and set a spell."

Danette was still seated on the Conestoga, her hands folded primly in her lap. Her eyes, in contrast, blazed with defiance as she slowly lowered herself to the ground.

"Seems we got us a wildcat with her claws tucked in," Eb joked.

"I'll clip 'em clean off if she gives us any grief," Justis threatened. He studied the five women before addressing the youngest, Catherine. "I figure you're the least likely to act up, missy, so I want you to go into each of these prairie boats of yours and bring out all the guns you have. And remember. I'll be checkin' later on, and if I find that you missed one, there'll be hell to pay."

Her features ashen, Catherine hurried to the last wagon.

"Easy as pie," Eb bragged. "Makes me wonder why this Orland jasper couldn't handle it himself." He glanced down at Fargo. "Or maybe he's right about you bein' a genuine curly wolf. The Trailsman, I think he called you. Is that right?"

Fargo merely nodded. Inwardly he wrestled with the renewed anguish in his head and restored his breathing to normal. He couldn't help but think of how swiftly he could turn the tables if only he had his Arkansas toothpick, and he wondered for the umpteenth time what had happened to the slender knife.

"Heard of you," Eb said, "but you don't look so tough to me. Maybe I'll test you later and find out."

"Leave him alone, you uncouth animal!" Susan snapped. "He's more man than both of you put together, and if you hadn't gotten the drop on him he'd make you sorry that you're taking blood money from a killer like Orland."

Eb snorted and poked his fellow hunter in the ribs. "Highfalutin', ain't she?"

"Maybe she's set her sights on this Trailsman feller," Justis jeered. "Must be why she thinks he's the best thing in britches since Adam." Strolling up to Susan, he touched a finger to her chin, and she angrily yanked backward. "You know, missy, I'm beginnin' to think you're right. I don't need that hundred dollars as much as I thought I did."

"What are you on about?" Eb said. "You know we're broke. How else are we goin' to get money?"

"I have me a notion," Justis said, puckering his lips. "Let it simmer a spell and I'll tell you once I work out all the details."

"There's no hurry. Orland and his crowd won't show for quite a while."

Their conversation was interrupted by the arrival of Catherine bearing four rifles and a pistol which she docilely deposited in front of them.

"You sort of remind me of a calf with those big round eyes of yours," Eb told her. His expression became lecherous. "And I love to eat calf meat."

Susan took a step, her fists partly raised. "Touch her and I'll kill you myself, you sons of bitches!"

"Such a mouth on a lady!" Eb retorted, and guffawed loudly. "But then, you ain't as ladylike as you let on, are you? Orland told us all about you, woman. So don't be takin' no airs with us. I won't stand for it."

Skye Fargo had deliberately not moved since being struck. And, as he'd hoped, the buffalo hunters had temporarily forgotten all about him as they bandied words with the women. He was next to Eb's legs. Beyond Eb stood Justis. There would never be a better time.

Steeling his muscles, Fargo hurled himself at the nearest hunter. His right shoulder slammed into Eb, who in turn stumbled sideways into Justis. Both men went down and Fargo was right there on top of them, his left fist catching Eb in the mouth even as he tore Eb's buffalo gun from the man's grasp and threw it aside. Eb was momentarily stunned, but under him Justis thrashed and squirmed to break free. Fargo took a short step, seizing Justis's rifle.

The scarred man clung tenaciously to it and lashed out with his right foot.

A biting pang exploded in Fargo's leg as it was knocked out from under him. He crashed onto the ground beside Justis, who had frantically wormed his way clear of Eb. Now, his face convulsed in savage blood lust, Justis grunted and snarled as he tried to rip his rifle from Fargo's unyielding grasp.

Abruptly, Justis let go and whipped out a big butcher knife. Teeth bared, he lunged. Had it not been for Fargo's superb reflexes the fight would have ended there. Fargo twisted, the glittering blade nicked his shirt, and he released the buffalo gun to grab his adversary's wrist.

"Damn your bones!" Justis fumed, seeking to wrench his arm loose.

Fargo knew better than to waste words while fighting for his life. His right knee arced up, catching the buffalo hunter in the chest. Once, twice, three times, and on the third blow Justis was flung backward, his knife arm bent at an unnatural angle. Fargo immediately applied pressure at the elbow. Justis vented a strident screech and allowed his knife to fall.

So intent was Fargo on the hunter with the scar that he neglected to keep an eye cocked on his other enemy, a mistake he appreciated fully when Eb pounced out of nowhere and bore him to the earth.

Fargo wound up flat on his back with Eb on top. Their fiery glares locked, and from the gap in Eb's teeth fell a drop of spittle that splattered on Fargo's cheek. Executing a supple but powerful heave, Fargo tossed the surprised hunter from him and shoved upright.

None too soon. Justis was already up and charging. He swung a crazed left cross that Fargo ducked under with ease. In return, Fargo stood Justis on his heels with a punch to the stomach. He drew back his other fist to wallop Justis again, but the cavalry arrived in the hurtling form of Eb, who slammed into Fargo from the side, once again bearing them both to the ground.

Jerking around, Fargo drove his elbow into Eb's face, and when Eb's head snapped back, he planted a fist on the hunter's jaw. Eb slumped, on the verge of unconsciousness. A single blow would finish him off so Fargo could deal with Justis. However, as Fargo braced to swing, he heard screams of warning from two or three of the ladies, and then a bull buffalo must have trampled on his head and crushed it because his skull seemed to explode into hundreds of pieces and a black void claimed him. His final thought before the darkness was simply, Not again!

7

Skye Fargo didn't want to wake up. He hovered on the brink of fully regaining his senses, resisting the flood of pain that threatened to burst the dam of his inner restraint and pour right through him if he woke. Then he felt a damp cloth on his forehead and a soft hand stroking his temple, and despite himself he opened his eyes. Instantly he regretted doing so. The pain was worse than he had anticipated, far worse than the last time. Dynamite went off between his ears, and he clutched at his head in torment.

"That bad, is it?" asked a kindly voice. "I wish we had some whiskey to give you. That might help."

Squinting up, Fargo discovered Susan Walker on her knees beside him. He blinked, looked away, and saw a blazing fire nearby. It took several moments for him to realize they were camped where the wagons had stopped, at the stand of trees. Across the fire sat the other four women, but there was no sign of the two buffalo hunters. "Where—?" he croaked.

"Don't talk unless it's absolutely necessary," Susan cautioned. "I thought Justis had killed you when he hit you with his gun. Then the other one beat on you a few times for good measure, he was so mad at the pounding you'd given him."

Clenching his teeth, Fargo eased his head down and sighed. "See if I ever stop in Abilene again," he grumbled.

Susan laughed, her hand straying to his broad shoulder. "It's a good sign when a person still has their sense of humor. You must have a remarkable constitution."

"No, just a hard head," Fargo said, and for a second had his agony blocked out by the shock he felt when Susan leaned over and, her back to her companions, kissed him lightly but fully on the mouth. Her lips briefly clung to his.

Then the moment passed, and she was her normal reserved self. "What was that for?" he asked.

"No special reason. Let's just say you remind me of my brother and let it go at that. It's safer for both of us that way."

Why is it women like to talk in riddles? Fargo wondered, gazing over her shoulder at the first Conestoga. Justis had just emerged bearing a number of frilly underthings which he now hoisted overhead as he whooped for joy.

"Eb, come see what I've found!"

Footsteps pounded from the direction of the other wagon and Eb appeared, his rifle cocked, his features grim. "What's that?" he asked. "Are they giving you a hard time again?"

"No, fool!" Justis replied, waving the underclothes. "Take a gander at these lace drawers. Did you ever imagine women wore such nonsense?"

"Is that all?" Eb snapped. "Damn you, I thought we were supposed to be seeing how many goods these women have, not pokin' around for playthings."

"And what did you find out?" Justis demanded stiffly.

"If I hadn't of seen it with my own eyes, I wouldn't believe it. They've crammed everything but an outhouse in there, and if they'd had more room they'd likely have brought one of those along, too."

"The same here," Justis said, a sly grin animating his swarthy features. "I was right, then? We're talkin' hundreds of dollars worth?"

"Maybe thousands."

"Thousands," Justis repeated, rolling the word on his tongue as if he was savoring every inflection. "Then it'd be worth it, wouldn't it? Especially if we get the askin' price for 'em."

"We'd be rich," Eb agreed.

"Go back and search proper. They might have money hid somewheres, in vases or jars and such."

"Or they might have a little gold," Eb said, his greed practically oozing from his pores. Cackling, he spun and returned to the second wagon.

Susan frowned and dipped the cloth in a pan of water. "I don't like the sound of that, not one bit." Her voice dropped to a whisper. "They've been rummaging in our wagons for fifteen minutes. Before that they were whisper-

71

ing and snickering together like a pair of naughty boys about to commit some vile prank."

"We've got to catch them when they come out again," Fargo proposed. He went to sit up but felt a curious tightening around his ankles, and looking down, he found his legs had been bound together with a stout piece of rope.

"Those beastly men did it," Susan explained the obvious. "Everyone has been tied except me, and the only reason I'm not is so I can be their pet servant. If they want coffee, I bring it. If they want food, I cook it. And since they're both busy at the moment, I figured I'd see what I could do for you."

Fargo was studying the multiple knots. He might be able to untie them, given ten minutes or so, but if he was caught in the act the buffalo hunters would stomp him into the dust. Since he was already bad enough off as it was, he decided to bide his time. "Can you get your hands on a knife?" he thought to ask.

"No. They won't let me take one out of the cabinet in my wagon. Spoons, yes. Forks, yes. Just no knives." Susan gently pressed the cloth to his brow again. "They're not quite as stupid as they appear to be."

"How are your friends holding up?"

"They're all nervous. Danette has been awful quiet, which as you know isn't like her at all. She certainly isn't afraid of them because she's never afraid of anything, so her attitude puzzles me."

Peering over the flames, Fargo saw the short woman with her arms resting on top of her bent knees. She was facing him, and smiled.

"What do you think they plan to do to us?" Susan inquired.

"They're supposed to keep you here until Orland catches up," Fargo reminded her.

"Somehow, I doubt they will."

Fargo silently agreed. He'd learned enough to know the hunters were entertaining grander plans, motivated by the money they stood to gain if they sold the Conestogas and all the possessions. And, ominously, the pair had hinted at also selling the women themselves, if he'd understood correctly.

Bell had been a fool to offer them the job, Fargo reflected, and Tom Orland had been a bigger fool to hire them. Buffalo hunters were a notoriously rowdy bunch who shunned civilization, preferring their own company as they wandered endlessly over the plains in search of their shaggy quarry. They were an independent, rugged bunch who never bothered with social niceties such as laws and polite manners. They went their own way and did as they damn well pleased.

Which, when Fargo thought about it, was exactly the personal philosophy he followed. But there any similarity ended. He could never bring himself to slaughter a score of buffalo at a time for a few coins in his pocket. If there was one lesson he'd learned from the Indians—and he'd learned many—it was to never waste game; never kill more than he could eat, never kill two animals for their skins if one was all he needed to make a new set of buckskins or whatever. This basic rule of survival was violated again and again by the buffalo hunters and others like them, so-called sportsmen, rich hunters who shot game for the sheer fun of it. He was as different from them as was day from night.

Fargo removed his hat and gingerly felt around his head. A knot the size of a walnut showed him where Justis had struck him. Close to it were more contusions, Eb's handiwork. If he kept going the way he was, pretty soon his head would resemble a bowl of hairy walnuts. The notion made him grin.

"You amaze me," Susan said softly. "How can you lie there and smile after all you've been through? From all the stories I'd heard, I expected you to be the type who eats nails for breakfast, wrestles grizzlies for exercise, and has the disposition of a castrated bull."

Fargo noticed that she had mentioned the bull without batting an eye. Curious, he brought up, "You still haven't told me how you know so much about my so-called reputation."

"A woman hears things. Why? Does it surprise you?"

"Most women don't hang around the sort of places where stories about me are told," Fargo mentioned, and relished the flush in her cheeks. "If the church-going crowd mentions my name, it's probably in the same breath with the Devil."

"You underrate yourself," Susan said defensively. "There are a lot of tales told about the good deeds you've done, the wagon trains you've guided through blizzards, the settlers you've helped in their fight against oppressors, the widows you've befriended."

Fargo remembered one particular widow and her lavish physical charms. "I had no idea I was such a saint," he remarked.

"Don't we have something much more important to discuss?" Susan asked.

"Such as?" Fargo responded, his now-lively lake-blue eyes roving over her attractive figure.

She paid him no mind. "Such as how we're going to escape the clutches of these horrid hunters and get away from Tom Orland?"

Whatever suggestions Fargo might have made were stilled by the appearance of Justis, who stepped onto the seat of the Conestoga, then jumped lightly to the ground. Rifle in hand, the buffalo hunter came toward them, an angry gleam in his dark eyes warning of his mood.

"All right, bitch! I've wasted enough time goin' through that wagon of yours. I know you have valuables in there, and I want to know where they are."

"You're sadly mistaken. We don't have anything you would want."

"Let me be the judge. Where is it?"

"There's a handbag containing two hundred dollars in the second wagon. That's all the money we own."

"Don't lie to me! It took a heap of dollars to buy all the pretty things you have. There must be more. Lots more."

Susan responded patiently. "We spent nearly every cent we owned to buy the wagons and our belongings. We wanted to have everything we'd need to start our new homes. Or didn't Orland tell you that we're on our way to Mountain City to be married?"

"Married?" Justis said, and laughed uproariously. "Don't that beat all." He scratched his beard. "Well, I reckon two hundred is better than nothing, and there will be a whole lot more before we're through." His attention shifted to the Trailsman and the cloth on Fargo's forehead. "Did I say you could doctor this bastard?" With a flick of his rifle, he knocked the cloth off, scraping Fargo's skin in the process.

Fargo was tempted to pounce then and there. A quick roll and he'd upend the hunter and possibly get his hands on the rifle. But Eb picked that moment to show, his tongue jutting through the space in his upper teeth as he hummed merrily.

"Why are you so happy?" Justis demanded.

"No reason. Can't a man just be grateful to be alive without someone givin' him a hard time?"

"Did you find anything?"

"Nothin'."

"No gold? No jewels? No money?" Justis asked, accenting the last word.

"Not a thing, I tell you. Maybe it's hid in the floorboards. We'll have to tear them up after we sell all the goods."

Fargo saw Justis finger the rifle. The scarred hunter was certain the toothless one was lying. What would Justis do? Kill Eb? Fargo hoped so, since that would reduce the odds considerably, and the moment Justis fired, Fargo would be on him like a wolf on a rabbit. He was disappointed, however, because all Justis did was scowl and turn away.

"What is this about selling our possessions?" Susan spoke up. "Tom Orland wouldn't like that."

"We don't much care what he likes, woman," Eb said. "We've been doin' some thinkin', and we see how we can come out rich men if we play this right."

"Yeah," Justis added, brightening at the prospect. "We're not beholden to that Orland gent. It's not like he's kin or anything. And he hasn't paid us a red cent yet."

"So commencin' at first light, we're headin' south across the prairie," Eb announced, raising his voice for the benefit of the other women. "If you all behave yourselves, you won't be harmed. But if you give us cause, we'll hurt you bad. Maybe peel a little skin off, or chop off one of your fingers or toes." He wiped the back of his hairy hand across his thick lips. "We won't kill you, though. The Comancheros don't pay for dead women."

Fargo had feared as much. The buffalo hunters were going to hand over Susan and the rest to the dreaded Comancheros, the notorious middlemen between the whites and the Comanches. He knew all about them.

Thanks to the many vicious raids the Comanches regularly conducted north and south of the Mexican border, the tribe had accumulated considerable plunder. And on both sides of the border there were certain unscrupulous Mexicans and whites who made hefty profits selling this booty back to their own countrymen. But since these unsavory characters were too afraid to deal with the Comanches directly, they hired the services of breeds, men born of mixed Indian-Mexican-white ancestry, to conduct the trade operations for them. These breeds were the Comancheros, and they were universally despised by everyone, even those who hired them.

Fargo had tangled with the Comancheros before. They were a savage, brutal bunch, more so at times than the Comanches from whom they stemmed. Comancheros were totally merciless, and would make the two gruff buffalo hunters seem like Sunday School teachers by comparison. If the women fell into their clutches, they'd end their days as virtual slaves of Comanche husbands. Comanches paid high prices for white women; having one as a wife was a symbol of the warrior's status.

"Please reconsider," Susan Walker was saying, her tone strained but level. "If you'll agree to help us reach Mountain City, I give you my word that you'll be paid five hundred dollars for your efforts by the men who are waiting for us there. And you won't have to worry about the law coming after you, as you will if you abduct us."

Justis sneered, then gestured at the surrounding plain. "Look around you, missy. You're miles from anywhere. There's no law out here, other than what a man carries." He wagged his rifle and tapped his Walker Colt. "Eb and me make our own laws."

"That's right," Eb said. "As for this Orland feller, I doubt he'll go cryin' to anyone once you turn up missin'. And we both know why." He chuckled. "Don't bother thinkin' he'll come after you, neither. His bunch is all city-bred. They ain't much good at trackin', I'll wager, and me and Justis have a few surprises up our sleeves that will leave 'em shakin' their heads and believin' the earth done swallowed you up."

The two buffalo hunters guffawed. Then Justis turned and jabbed the Trailsman with his foot. "But what about this polecat? The Comancheros wouldn't have no use for him."

"We kill him," Eb declared, and started to pull Fargo's Colt from under his belt.

"No. Wait," Justis said. "Not like that. It'd be too easy."

"What do you have in mind, then?"

"How about if we have us a few laughs with this *hombre*

76

come sunup?" Justis responded, and tittered. "Just like we did that time with those Arapahos?"

"Now there's an idea!" Eb agreed with delight. "I'd forgot all about those bucks and squaws. And a man can always use some target practice."

Fargo was staring at the knife strapped to Justis's waist. If only he could get his hands on it, he reflected. He tensed his legs, testing to see if he could lunge very far with his ankles bound as they were. But a rifle barrel suddenly swung down to within an inch of his eyes, causing him to freeze.

"Don't be gettin' no ideas, Trailsman," Justis declared. "Eb, tie this varmint's hands so he won't be actin' up during the night."

Unable to resist, Fargo was pushed onto his side and had his arms jerked behind his back. Then he was trussed with another length of rope taken from one of the wagons. Eb derived pleasure from making the loops and the knots as tight as he could.

"There! This would hold a buffalo."

"What about us?" Susan asked indignantly. "Surely you're not going to tie us up like that?"

"As a matter of fact, we are," Justis said. "Just as soon as you've all ate. We wouldn't want you to starve yourselves on our account. The Comancheros don't much like skinny women."

The buffalo hunters thought that hilarious.

Fargo had seldom felt so helpless as he did lying there and watching the miserable women pick at their food under the gloating gazes of Justis and Eb. The pair took particular pleasure in taunting their captives and made a number of remarks about the physical charms of each one. All five women refused to dignify the comments with a response, and after a while the hunters lost interest.

Once the meal was done, Justis covered the ladies while Eb tied their hands. He was far more gentle than he had been with Fargo. Often he contrived to brush a hand against a jutting breast or a soft thigh. By the time he was done, sweat beaded his face and he kept licking his lips as if he were dying of thirst.

The only one who had a comment to make was Susan Walker. "This wasn't necessary. What harm would it do to let us sleep inside where we can be more comfortable?"

"We want you where we can keep an eye on all of you at once," Eb answered. "Although," and he smirked, "the notion of bein' tucked all nice and cosy in one of them wagons with you by my side is right nice."

Susan fell silent.

It was Justis, surprisingly, who went into the wagons and brought out blankets to cover each woman. Then he sat down with his partner and polished off the coffee.

Fargo shut out their mindless chatter and took stock of his predicament. He didn't know what the two hunters had planned for him in the morning, but he could safely bet it would be something brutal, even fiendish. They were crafty in their own way, and had no compunctions about how they killed.

Fargo remembered them saying something about Arapahos and wondered what they had meant. Abruptly, unbidden, a recollection of the Broken Butte mystery, as it was called when the story was told in saloons and around campfires, jarred his memory. A few years back a scout for the army had come across the darnedest sight: a string of five dead Arapahos, two old men and three women, lying in a line from east to west, their bodies spaced about ten yards apart. Each one had been shot in the back of the head, except a single warrior who had been shot twice in the face. No one had ever claimed credit for the killings, and the tribe was still seeking information on the culprits. Could it have been Justis and Eb?

Fargo forced himself to relax and closed his eyes. He'd need his wits about him in the morning. Sleep was essential, no matter how worked up he was. But he found it easier to think about resting than to actually drift off. His mind was going hell for leather, and no matter what he did he couldn't rein it in. Resigned to the inevitable, he thought about the women and what he would like to do if he somehow lived through the next day. They were all good-looking in their own way, yet he favored Susan Walker. Although she was always so reserved and proper, he sensed that beneath her surface lurked a smoldering volcano just waiting for the right man to come along and burst her lava. So to speak.

The fire dwindled lower and lower. Coyotes yipped in the distance. Once an owl asked who was there. The buffalo hunters took turns sleeping. Justis had the first watch, Eb the second. Each, in turn, sat huddled close to the flames for warmth, a heavy buffalo robe over his shoulders, his rifle held between his legs so he could grasp it quickly should hostiles attack.

In the wee hours of the night Fargo finally did fall into an uneasy sleep. He tossed and shifted, in the grip of nightmare visions of lead balls coring his brain or ripping through his body. When he awoke shortly before dawn, a fine layer of clammy perspiration caked his skin.

The buffalo hunters were both on their feet well before daylight. Eb kindled the fire while Justis brought bread and eggs from the first wagon. All the women were slumbering, except for Danette.

Fargo first noticed her when he scanned the five of them and saw her eyes were open. Danette gave a slight bob of her chin, as if nodding at her dress. When his brow knit in confusion, she did it again. He had no idea what she was trying to tell him, and careful not to be seen by the hunters, he shrugged. She frowned, then pretended to be asleep when Justis came near her.

The first golden rays were painting the eastern sky when Eb cupped a hand to his grizzled mouth and whooped, "Rise and shine, ladies! We got us a heap of travelin' to do today after breakfast."

Justis cut Susan loose and pointed at the pot. "Get to work, missy. We ain't about to cook for ourselves with womenfolk present. Fix us eggs and make 'em tasty."

Rising, Susan rubbed her sore wrists and scowled. "I will if you untie my friends first."

"You'll do it anyway," Justis declared. "But to show you I ain't the bastard you think, I'll untie their hands. How would that be?"

Susan put her hands on her hips and glared defiantly at the scarred hunter. "I refuse. Cut their legs free, too. This treatment is inhuman, and you know we're not going to try and run off."

"You don't seem to understand something here, missy," Justis said, and gave her a ringing slap across the face. Susan staggered but stayed on her feet, a hand over her cheek. "We tell *you* what to do. You don't tell us," he snarled. "And if you give me cause again, I'll slice some hide off one of you for sure. Now fix the damn food!"

"That's tellin' her!" Eb said.

Justis turned, his furious gaze falling on Fargo. "Don't worry, mister. We ain't forgotten about you. As soon as we're done eatin', we're goin' to see if the high and mighty Trailsman bleeds just like ordinary folks." And with that, for no reason at all, he gave Fargo a kick in the ribs. "Yes, sir. This will be fun!"

8

The pain in Skye Fargo's ribs had subsided by the time the hunters wolfed down their eggs and coffee and turned their attention back to him. They each grabbed hold under an arm and dragged him a dozen yards from the fire, to the edge of the grass on the north side of the rutted trail. Here they left him for a while.

Fargo had been trying to loosen the rope around his wrists, but to no avail. Both wrists were chafed and torn, and he could feel blood trickling along his left forearm. His only hope lay in the character of the buffalo hunters. As brutal as they were, they weren't the kind to simply shoot him as he lay there helpless. What "fun" would they get out of that? They must have something else in mind, some way that he would provide them with a little entertainment. Whatever it was, they might have to cut him loose. And if they did that, no matter how slim the prospects, he at least stood a fighting chance of surviving.

This was the slim straw of hope to which Fargo clutched as he watched the hunters go from woman to woman, untying their ankles. Eb stood back and covered them while Justis goaded them over to the wagon, where they were lined up facing the prairie.

Susan Walker held herself as proudly as ever. Catherine and Rita, the two youngest, were slumped in despair. Audris appeared petrified. And Danette, oddly, stood as calmly as could be, her hands at her sides.

"Now then," Justis declared, "we don't want none of you kickin' up a fuss once we get started. Just pay attention, and remember that what happens to the Trailsman could well happen to you if you push us too far."

"Let's get this over with," Eb urged. "That Orland feller might change his mind and show up sooner than we figure. We've got a lot to do yet."

"Hold your britches on," Justis said. Drawing his butcher knife, he grinned in anticipation and walked toward Fargo. "We did this to some Arapahos a while back," he mentioned as he crouched and touched the blade to the rope binding Fargo's arms. "Since I hear tell that you lived with Injuns once, it's fittin' you're goin' to die like those worthless red savages did."

Fargo flinched as the knife was slashed right through the rope and into his skin, opening a cut an inch long.

"Look at that! Now how could I have been so careless?" Justis gave the rope securing Fargo's legs the same treatment, then stood, jammed his knife into its beaded sheath, and hefted his rifle. "On your feet, mister."

Slowly, Fargo did as they wanted. He had to prop his hands under him and push up until he was doubled over and swaying as if drunk. The movement had sparked a sharp tingling sensation in both of his legs, brought on by the lack of circulation.

Justis backed up a few feet. "When we did this with them mangy Arapahos, we made a game out of it. We let one go ten yards, then shot her dead. Then we let the next one go twenty yards and did the same. And on and on. By the time we were done, we had the prettiest row of good Injuns you ever did see." He paused. "But since there's just one of you, I'll have to do this a mite different." His arm jabbed at the plain. "You head out across that grassland just as fast as you can run. And when I'm ready, I'm going to start taking pieces out of you a shot at a time until you're on your way to hell. Try to make it interestin'. Weave like a jackrabbit if you want. Go to ground if you'd like. It won't matter. I'm a crack shot, Trailsman. I can blow the eye out of a buffalo at two hundred yards."

Fargo didn't doubt it. Any man who used a gun often enough eventually became fairly proficient, and buffalo hunters relied on their rifles day in and day out. Gritting his teeth, he managed to straighten and took a wobbly step.

"Take your time," Justis baited him. "I don't want this to be too easy."

By lifting first one leg and then the other, Fargo got his blood flowing properly again. His ankles hurt, but he could move well enough to run. He surveyed the prairie, seeking somewhere to take cover; it was open and flat for as far as the eye could see. A bird couldn't hide out there, let alone a man.

"You look ready to me," Justis said. "So off you go."

Fargo glanced at the grimy hunter, suppressing an impulse to charge recklessly. He took a step, on the verge of racing for his life, when an ear-splitting shriek rent the cool morning air. Startled, he turned and saw Danette flying toward him like a demented banshee, her arms waving wildly, her head tossed back as she screamed her lungs out.

The buffalo hunters were equally shocked. Both were gaping at her in amazement, too stunned to intervene.

Before Fargo quite guessed her intent, Danette plowed into him, knocking him off his feet. He felt her arms go around his waist as he fell, and then he landed, hard, and her lips were on his mouth, his cheek, his ear. "Underneath you!" she whispered urgently, and went on kissing him feverishly.

"What the hell!" Justis recovered his faculties. In a stride, he reached them and seized Danette by the shoulder. "Get off him, damn you!" He yanked her erect and sent her stumbling backward.

Fargo stayed on the ground. Both hunters had forgotten all about him for the moment. Quickly, he slipped a hand under his back and felt in the grass until his fingers brushed a hard, slender object. As he grasped it he recognized the shape. Danette had slipped him a knife, but not just any knife. He'd held this one often enough to know it was his own Arkansas toothpick, and he glanced at her in surprise, trying to deduce how she had gotten her hands on the weapon. He'd finally figured Orland had taken it after pistol-whipping him back in Abilene.

Danette stood with her face scarlet and her bosom heaving, a sly smile creasing her mouth.

"What the hell was that all about?" Justis exploded. "Were you tryin' to get yourself shot?"

"I had to kiss him one last time," Danette replied.

"One last—?" Justis said, and did a double take. "You mean him and you? But I thought it was him and that other filly?"

Her face as impassive as marble, Danette coolly lied, "It's both of us."

"Well, I'll be damned!"

During this exchange Fargo had sat up. By shielding his

arms with his body so no one could see, he'd slipped the toothpick up his right sleeve, leaving the hilt in his palm. Now, his fingers curled up to hold the knife in place and his arm at his side so the hunters wouldn't notice the unusual way he was holding his hand, he slowly rose.

Justis looked at him. "You sure do beat all, mister. It's almost a shame to have to kill a man who has such a winnin' way with the ladies. But we've got to do it." He motioned at Danette. "All right, missy. You had your kiss. Get over by the wagon and behave yourself."

Rather haughtily, Danette did as she was told, but not until she had blown Skye a kiss.

"Women are such strange critters," Justis declared. Then he swung around, his rifle as steady as a rock. "Let's get this over with. I don't have all day."

Fargo hesitated. He estimated he was ten feet from Justis, within easy killing range of his throwing knife. Yet even if his toss was true, he couldn't possibly cover the forty feet to Eb before a bullet stopped him. If he knew that he could count on the women to help, to jump Eb once Justis was down, he would have made the attempt. But three of the five were in no condition to lend a hand, and Danette and Susan wouldn't be able to overpower Eb on their own without being gravely hurt, or worse. He had no choice.

"I'm waitin'," Justis prompted.

Fargo started running. But he did so slowly, his head swiveled so he would know when Justis was about to fire.

"Faster!" the hunter demanded.

Despite the command, Fargo continued to run slowly. He was counting on Justis to hold fire until he had gone a certain distance. The longer it took him to go that far, the more time he had to think, to scheme.

"Faster, I said!"

Fargo had gone ten yards. He picked up the pace a fraction, fighting off a wave of panic. Had he made a mistake he wouldn't live to regret? he wondered. Should he have jumped Justis when he was closer and hoped for the best with Eb? Another five yards fell behind him, and there wasn't so much as a shallow rut in the ground for him to flatten in when the time came.

Which it did, seconds later. Justis smirked and tucked the rifle to his shoulder.

At any instant Fargo could expect to have the slug tear

through him. He was as close to death as he had ever been, and in desperation he did the only thing he could think of, relying on a ruse that was old when the hills were new. Yet the men he was dealing with weren't the brightest around. They took everything literally. So when he abruptly whirled, pointed at the stand of trees, and screamed in feigned fear, "Behind you, ladies! Indians!" the two buffalo hunters did as he wanted; they spun to confront the presumed danger.

In a twinkling Skye Fargo was off, sprinting northward like an antelope, his long legs bounding a yard and a half with each stride. Five precious seconds the ruse gave him. Then seven. He glanced over his shoulder just as an enraged Justis turned and took a bead on his back.

"You tricky son of a bitch! I'll fix you!"

Fargo flung his arms out and dived. He was in midair when the rifle boomed. There was no concussion, no agony. The bullet had missed. As Fargo came down, he rolled to the left, into a crouch, and saw Justis reloading. Unbending, Fargo ran as a rabbit would, zigzagging constantly. Ten additional yards fell under his flying feet. A check showed Justis taking aim once more, and on seeing that, Fargo threw himself to the left. He heard the retort of the rifle and something snatched at his sleeve but didn't break the buckskin or his own hide.

Onward Fargo fled. The grass was up to his knees, but he knew he was still too close to the hunters to try hiding in it. They'd distinguish the outline of his body by the manner in which the tops of the blades were pushed aside. He had to gain more distance.

Justis was fumbling with a new cartridge. His single-shot breech loader was too heavy and unwieldy to be fired rapidly, and he was complicating matters with his haste.

Fargo went straight to cover more ground that much more swiftly. He saw Justis raise the rifle. Darting to the right, he hurled himself into the grass as the rifle thundered. The buzz of the bullet told him how narrowly he had escaped.

Instead of rising right away, Fargo snaked to the right, his arms and legs churning. Justis would be concentrating on the spot where he had gone to ground, and it would take a few seconds for the oaf to realize Fargo was shifting position. Justis would then spot the moving grass and get set to squeeze off his next shot the moment Fargo popped up. Which was exactly what Fargo wanted.

A fist-sized clump of bluestem gave Fargo the means to foil the hunter yet again. Pausing, he wrenched on the clump, tearing it loose. The toothpick severed the roots. Then he crawled another ten feet to give Justis plenty of time to mark his position. Halting, he drew his arm down to his side, tensed, and threw the clump on high.

Justis fell for the ploy. The buffalo gun blasted. The clump dissolved in a shower of grass and dirt.

And Fargo was up and off again, sprinting all out, the fiery curses of the enraged hunter music to his ears. Eb was bellowing for Justis to hurry it up, that Fargo was getting too far off, proving Eb had more brains than his companion. Another fifteen or twenty yards and Fargo could safely go to ground again, since the hunters wouldn't be able to tell if the grass was pushed aside or not from that distance. They would have to come after him.

One more time, Justis reloaded the rifle and pressed the stock to his shoulder.

Fargo was watching. He twisted to the right, to the left, to the right again, conscious of a prickling sensation rippling down his spine. But no shot came. Justis was holding his fire, wanting to be certain he didn't miss. As soon as Fargo tired and slowed, the fatal shot would sound. But Fargo wasn't about to foolishly exhaust himself. He suddenly halted and spun, extending his right arm toward Justis, the Arkansas toothpick clasped in his fingers at such an angle that the shiny steel blade reflected the brilliant sunlight like a mirror. The result was more than he could have hoped for.

"Look out! He's got a gun!" Eb screamed, and both buffalo hunters promptly sank low.

Fargo would have laughed if he hadn't been busy running. He bought himself another twenty seconds. When Justis warily stood, he went prone. Angling to the left, he covered eight or nine yards when, without warning, he pushed through a screen of grass and tumbled headfirst down an incline. His first thought was that he had stumbled on a buffalo wallow, but when he came to rest on his side and glanced around, he discovered he was lying in a shallow gully rimmed by high grass. The perfect hiding place.

Clutching the knife close to his chest, Fargo lay still and waited. There were shouts, but the words were indistinct. Minutes dragged by, and then the clomp of hoofs alerted him to the approach of one of the hunters on horseback. He didn't budge. Since much of the surrounding grass was brown, his buckskins blended into the background. The man would have to be right on him before he was spotted.

It was Justis, as an angry shout proved. "I don't know where the hell he is! And quit naggin' me, damn you! I can't hear a thing with you squawkin'."

The thud of hoofs grew closer. Fargo listened for the sound of the animal's breathing; that would tell him Justis was close enough to see him. Yet although the horse criss-crossed the immediate vicinity for the next five minutes, it never came quite that near.

Presently Justis called out. "Tie those women up and get your carcass over here! I need your help."

Eb answered, but his reply was lost on the wind.

Fargo heard Justis spit out a string of curses. For five more minutes the horse circled, then the hunter galloped off, toward the wagons. Suspecting a ruse, Fargo stayed down low. After a while he heard a faint shout. There was nothing else for the longest time, then a whinny. Overcome by curiosity, Fargo rose on his knees, inched to the top of the gully, and parted the grass, careful not to expose his head.

The Conestogas were rolling southward across the prairie. They were being driven by the women while the buffalo hunters rode on either side of the wagons. Tied to the back of the second wagon was the Ovaro.

Fargo hadn't anticipated this happening. He'd figured on the hunters conducting a thorough search of the area, and once he'd lured them both out in the grass where there was little likelihood of the women being hit by a stray bullet, he would have shown them a few things he'd learned from the Indians they despised so much. Now his plan was ruined. Worse, they were leaving him afoot in the middle of the Plains, a fate every horseman dreaded.

Flattening himself on the ground, Fargo made for the trail. At regular intervals he would rise high enough to mark the progress of the wagons and ensure neither of the hunters had turned around. The Conestogas were almost a mile off when he saw the smoldering remains of the fire, and stood. Hastening forward, he grabbed a stick and poked at the embers, uncovering several burning coals. He applied grass and twigs until tiny flames lapped at the tinder, then added pieces of broken branches and shortly had the fire going again.

Fargo squatted on his haunches and took stock. The reason most travelers feared being stranded afoot in the midst of the virtually limitless wilderness was because so few knew how to live off the land. It never ceased to amaze him how many pilgrims would venture into the unknown without the slightest idea of how to go about finding food and water. If not for their supplies, they would die. And many did just that when they became lost or when their wagons broke down and their provisions ran out, as the countless crude graves lining the various trails westward testified.

The Trailsman wasn't so easily defeated, by man or nature. He had a knife and his knowledge of the wild, and with them he would survive long enough to catch up to Justis and Eb and have his revenge. Accordingly, he stood and entered the stand of trees. A short search uncovered a long, stout limb ideal for his purpose. He carried it to the fire, trimmed off the thin offshoots, and worked at sharpening the thicker end for the next fifteen minutes. When he had a point that would penetrate the thick hide of a buffalo, he held it over the flames, charring the exposed inner wood until it was rock hard.

Now Fargo had a knife and a serviceable spear. But he wasn't through. Going back into the trees, he inspected a score of slender limbs until he found one to his liking. Supple and strong, it would do admirably. He chopped it off at the base with the toothpick, then sliced off a small knob and several tiny branches, making the limb smooth.

Back at the fire, Fargo carved notches in the two ends and hardened them over the fire as he had done the spear. Next he methodically cut whangs off his buckskin shirt, ten in all, and tied these thin strips of fringe into one long piece. Taking the slender limb, he knotted one end of his makeshift cord to the top and the other end to the bottom, first bending the limb enough to give it a pronounced curve. When he was done, he held a crude but effective bow in his hands.

Since a bow without arrows was worthless, Fargo went among the trees collecting ten thin, straight branches. These were likewise trimmed, sharpened, and hardened. Since he lacked the means to add fletching at the moment, the range of his arrows would be limited, but they would work fine if he came on small game.

Thus armed, Fargo extinguished the fire and walked along the stand until he came to where the new trail the wagons had made should be. Here he was surprised to find the grass had been bent back up into place to disguise the exact point at which the wagons had left the established trail. The buffalo hunters, Fargo deduced, had used branches as rakes to hide the spot so that when Orland came along later, he wouldn't notice. Orland would think the wagons had kept on heading west. Pretty clever for a pair of yacks, Fargo mused.

The Arkansas toothpick had already gone into the sheath on his ankle. The bow Fargo now slung over his left shoulder. With the spear in his right hand and the arrows in his left, he broke into a dog trot, starting his pursuit. The Conestogas had disappeared over the horizon, but the flattened path of grass they'd made was easy to follow.

Overhead the hot Kansas sun beat down. Fargo maintained a steady pace, slowing frequently to conserve his strength. His goal was to get the wagons in sight again, then shadow them until nightfall, at which time he would spring a surprise on Justis and Eb.

The scent of the grass and the warmth of the sun on Fargo's face and back brought up memories of a summer spent with the Sioux. He remembered running through the high buffalo grass with a sweet maiden, and the passion of their coupling beside a gurgling stream. He recalled going on a buffalo hunt with the warriors, and the thrill of the subsequent chase.

Occasionally the wind would gust, rustling the grass. Insects buzzed. A lone hawk soared overhead in a circle, rose, and sailed away.

Then, for half an hour or more, Fargo was the only moving thing in all the vast prairie. Sweat trickled down his back and his feet began to ache, but he ignored both discomforts. He did pull his hat brim lower over his eyes to shield them from the sun.

A small herd of antelope materialized to the west. They were hundreds of yards off and seemed to sense he was no danger to them because they simply stood and watched him go by instead of fleeing.

The tiny white blob had been framed on the horizon for

a while before Fargo realized he was looking at the top of the last Conestoga. He fell into a steady walk, scouring the plain for signs of the two hunters. If they were smart, one or the other would always be scouting a ways off from the wagons, keeping an eye out for hostiles. He saw no one.

Fargo was growing tired of holding all the arrows. His palm was slippery with perspiration and they shifted often, once almost slipping from his grasp. To free his hand, he stopped and slid them one at a time down the back of his shirt. The notched ends stuck out to one side of his head. To grasp one, all he had to do was reach back.

To be safe, Fargo allowed the wagons to increase their lead a slight margin before he resumed trailing them. He didn't care to have the hunters accidentally catch sight of him. Off to the left he spied a buffalo chip. Beyond it were more. A herd must have passed by within the past few days, he reflected, continuing on.

Fargo was abreast of the scattered chips when from the grass on his right there came a low rumbling sound. He drew up short, both hands gripping the spear. The rumbling was repeated, as if whatever was making the noise was annoyed, and was punctuated by a loud grunt. Fargo crouched low, hoping against hope he hadn't been detected. But he had, as was demonstrated seconds later when an enormous dark form stood up and regarded him balefully.

It was a massive bull buffalo.

9

Skye Fargo didn't twitch a muscle. To do so, to make any sudden moves at all, might invite a charge. He stared at the bull, waiting for it to show its intentions, his stout spear suddenly seeming puny in comparison to the huge, muscular bulk of the lord of the plains.

Buffalo were notoriously unpredictable. Like humans, they all reacted differently to similar sets of circumstances. Where one would attack at the sight of an enemy, another might flee. Bulls were generally more belligerent than cows, but here again there was no set pattern. Both were extremely dangerous when aroused, as many a buffalo hunter had found out the hard way.

Fargo wanted to do nothing that would arouse this one. He couldn't understand what it was doing there all by itself, since by their very nature buffalo were sociable creatures that liked to congregate in herds. There was no such thing as a "loner" buffalo. Occasionally, when one became too old to keep up with the herd, it would fall far behind and eventually be brought down by wolves. Or a cow might temporarily be left if a herd moved on while she was giving birth. But a buffalo wandering the prairie on its own was unheard of.

So Fargo studied the brute before him, seeking an explanation for its presence, and he found the reason almost immediately. Jutting from the left shoulder was the feathered end of an arrow. From the flank protruded two more, one broken off. Now he understood. The herd to which this bull had belonged had been set on by an Indian hunting party, perhaps Cheyenne or Arapaho, and during the ensuing chase the bull had been shot three times but not gone down. Which wasn't at all remarkable. Often wounded buffalo would run for miles before dropping. Unless a shot was precisely placed, it was seldom fatal. Fargo knew of instances where hunters had shot particular animals ten times or more and still failed to stop them.

The knowledge was not comforting. Wounded buffalo were even more dangerous. Fargo watched its hindquarters, since the first sign a bull often gave of an impending charge was a sudden flick upward of its tufted tail. But the bull just stood there, staring.

Sweat trickled from under Fargo's hat, across his brow, and into his eyes. His left eye began to smart, yet he dared not lift an arm to wipe it. The burning increased, and then the right eye started in. Fargo involuntarily blinked.

Uttering a bellicose snort, the bull snapped its tail erect, lowered its enormous head, and thundered forward.

Fargo back-pedaled, the tip of his spear held straight out from his chest. He might as well be using a twig. If the bull struck him head-on, the spear would be reduced to kindling in a second. And once his spear was gone, he'd be defenseless. His other weapons would have no more effect on such a monster than would a slingshot.

As the bull narrowed the distance, Fargo balanced on the balls of his feet and tensed his legs. The bull, he had noticed, was moving sluggishly, at a third of the speed it was capable of achieving. One of the arrows in its side had either hit a vital organ, or else ripped open a vein and caused internal bleeding. Whatever, this bull was a shadow of its usual self, and on this Fargo hinged his chances of living to see the next sunset.

Fargo glued his gaze to the bull's head, to those wicked curved horns with their three-foot spread. When the bull came close enough, it would slash to the right and left, trying to hook him and gore him. He must be ready.

The buffalo was wheezing like an out-of-control steam engine, its powerful hoofs sending clumps of earth flying in its wake. Its great hump bobbed as it charged, like the humps of whales did when they crested the surface of the ocean, as Fargo had once seen them do off the coast of California.

Ten yards separated the shaggy giant from the Trailsman. Fargo's every nerve was on fire. His mind shrieked at him to run, to flee, but he stayed rooted in place until the bull was so close he could see its nostrils flaring and drops of saliva rimming its mouth. Then he twisted and sprang to the left. In his ear was the pounding of hoofs. Something nicked his shirt. He came down on his knees and scrambled around to see the bull thirty feet away and turning.

Fargo pushed upright and braced for the next rush. The spear was in his right hand, raised high. He had to do more than dodge the bull's repeated attacks if he wanted to live; eventually he'd slip or make some other mistake and the buffalo would trample him. He must fight back in the only way possible.

The bull stumbled but promptly recovered, dug in its hoofs, and barreled toward him, breathing louder than before.

Once Fargo had seen a Sioux warrior do what he was about to do, when the warrior had been unhorsed during a buffalo surround and set on by an irate cow. The Sioux had only partially succeeded. The cow had clipped him, tearing his shoulder apart. Fargo had to be faster or there would be a similar outcome.

Head held low, the bull came on at a lurching trot. Fargo gauged the gap carefully, and when the bull's ponderous head was less than two yards from him he leaped to the right while simultaneously hurling his spear with all the strength in his shoulder and arm. The charred point caught the buffalo in the hairy folds of its neck and sank in deep. At the very same instant, the bull whipped its head around.

Fargo saw the horn sweeping in his direction and was helpless to prevent it from slamming into him. A tremendous pain erupted in his chest. He was lifted from the ground as if by an invisible hand and propelled a dozen feet through the air. His back bore the jolting impact. He winced as several of his arrows gouged into his skin. Afraid the bull would be on him again before he could stand, Fargo shoved up and spun.

The bull had stopped and was swaying, its head cocked at an odd angle, blood pouring from the wound in its neck.

Fargo looked down at his shirt. The horn had torn the buckskin, but not his flesh. Though his ribs were aflame with pain, he didn't think any were broken. Quickly he unslung the bow and pulled an arrow out. As he nocked the shaft to the string, he saw the bull shuffle toward him and he started to retreat since he doubted whether his crude arrow could penetrate its thick hide. Then the bull tripped and fell forward, its front legs bent. Grunting and thrashing, it struggled to rise but couldn't.

Suddenly Fargo threw caution to the wind and raced toward the buffalo, lifting his bow as he did. This was his golden opportunity. The bull bellowed and increased its frantic efforts, in vain. It was too weak to raise its mammoth form. Fargo ran right up to its head, pulled the arrow back as far as the string would allow, took deliberate aim, and sent the shaft into the buffalo's wide eye.

The bull jarred upward and voiced a rasping bellow. Jerking convulsively, it flailed its head from side to side. A pink froth poured from its parted lips.

Fargo had backed off to avoid those slashing horns. He notched a second shaft, but it wasn't needed. The bull's movements became weaker and weaker, its bellows reduced to feeble grunts, and at length, uttering a drawn-out sigh, it rolled slowly over onto its side and was still.

Lowering his bow, Fargo sank down in the grass and took deep breaths, which helped ease some of the pain in his chest. He stared at the massive bull, amazed at his luck. Had he been an inch closer to it when it struck him, he wouldn't have risen again.

A check of the southern horizon showed the Conestogas were long gone. They would be easy to overtake, though, since Justis and Eb would have to stop for the night to rest the mules and their horses. Fargo had some time to spare. That, and the dead buffalo, gave him an idea on how he could put part of the beast to good use. Drawing the Arkansas toothpick, he rose.

For the next hour Fargo worked diligently, stripping the hide from the carcass. Since he didn't intend to make a robe out of it, he did a rough job, taking shortcuts where possible and leaving on parts of the hide he would have removed otherwise. With a Bowie or butcher knife the task would have taken half as long, but the toothpick sufficed.

Once Fargo had the hide off, he spread it out flat on the ground with the hairy side on the bottom. It would defeat his purpose if the hide hardened and became too stiff to manage, so, with the aid of his spear, he was able to make an opening at the back of the bull's skull and extract the brains. These he rubbed all over the inner surface of the hide, mashing the lumps to the consistency of a sticky paste, to keep the hide supple.

After hacking off a large piece of meat to eat later, Fargo rolled it in the hide and slung the whole thing over his left shoulder. He had his bow over his other shoulder. To his arrow collection he had added the two good shafts taken from the bull. Stooping to retrieve his spear, he turned and took a step. And halted in consternation.

A large pack of gray wolves had silently converged as he worked and were now arranged in a semi-circle thirty feet off. Some were standing, others sitting. Most had their pinkish tongues lolling out. At the forefront stood the biggest male, its unblinking eyes fixed on the Trailsman.

Fargo knew better than to let them think he was in any way afraid. Long ago he'd learned that once an animal sensed or smelled fear, it was far more likely to attack. Tightening his hold on the spear, he advanced straight toward them, toward the leader. Several of the wolves snarled. A few whined. Most moved quickly aside, forming an aisle through their midst. Only one or two stood their ground, and one of those was the big male.

Ordinarily wolves were wary of humans and went out of their way to avoid conflict. Fargo counted on that fact as he strode purposefully nearer. He'd heard of three or four instances in which packs had attacked trappers or hunters, but always in the lean of winter when the packs were invariably half-starved. This pack appeared fairly well-fed.

The leader didn't move until Fargo was close enough to jab it with the spear. Then, in a burst of speed, the big wolf darted around him and dashed to the carcass. This was the signal for all the wolves to fall in a feeding frenzy on the buffalo, and in the blink of a eye the carcass was covered with snapping, growling figures.

Fargo hiked southward. The sun was high now, the heat intense. He conserved his energy for later, when he would really need it. Twice during the long afternoon he stopped to cut small chunks of meat from the steak and pop the raw morsels in his mouth. Rather than chew them, he sucked on the meat so he would salivate and keep his mouth and throat moist.

Toward evening a line of trees appeared. Trees meant water, and Fargo increased his pace. He sought some sign of the Conestogas but it appeared the buffalo hunters had kept on going. Appearances, however, could be deceiving, as Fargo discovered when he was fifty feet from the trees and a soft whinny reached his ears.

Without bothering to pinpoint the source, Fargo dropped

to the ground and set the hide down. Off to the west grew an isolated cluster of thin cottonwoods ringed by dense brush. From the center of this plot a tiny spiral of smoke rose, dissipating in the branches overhead. Justis and Eb had stopped after all.

Fargo grabbed the hide and crawled to his left, away from the campsite. He soon reached the higher grass bordering the water, a trickle of a stream two feet wide and four inches deep. Glancing upstream, he spied one of the women filling a pot. It was Danette. He rose on an elbow to wave, then dropped flat when Eb strolled into view, a rifle hooked in the crook of his elbow. Eb addressed Danette. She, in turn, spun and gave him a tongue lashing. Fargo couldn't hear the words but her gestures were obvious. Eb only laughed.

Soon the pair walked off. Fargo inched to the stream and eagerly lowered his face, relishing the cool sensation as the water played over his hot face. He gulped greedily, then drew back and wiped his eyes so he could scan the area west of him. As much as he wanted to sneak closer to see if all the women were safe, he curbed his impatience and moved back under a high bush to await nightfall.

Fargo had planned to eat the meat before dark, but he couldn't start a fire so close to the buffalo hunters. Filling his belly would have to wait. He stored the rolled hide at the base of the bush and used it as a pillow as he reclined on his back. A short rest was in order so he would be refreshed and alert when it came time to try and free the women from the clutches of Justis and Eb. Closing his eyes, he allowed himself to drift off, counting on his inner clock to wake him well before midnight.

It did. By the position of the Big Dipper, Fargo guessed it was nine o'clock when he sat up and stretched. A tranquil veil of darkness shrouded the still prairie. The wind had stopped, so even the grass was quiet for once.

Coarse laughter came from the direction of the Conestogas. Fargo rose and went to the stream for a quick drink. Then, hugging the edge of the water where the ground was soft and his footsteps were muffled, he glided through the night until he spied a glimmer of firelight through the brush. Dipping low, he worked his way into the undergrowth, parting branches with exquisite care and crawling where necessary.

The buffalo hunters had a roaring fire going. Everything within a dozen yards was brightly illuminated, and a weaker golden glow extended much farther. Fargo had to watch that he didn't get too close. From forty feet away he studied the layout of the camp.

One of the wagons was north of the fire, the other to the south. A rope corral had been formed to prevent the mules and the horses from straying off, and as an added precaution the Ovaro was tied to the north wagon. The five women were seated in a row near the flames, while across from them, each taking a turn sipping from a whiskey bottle, sat their captors.

Fargo couldn't hear what was being said. As near as he could tell, the two men were baiting the women, trying to get them to drink, but the ladies adamantly refused. He saw Justis thrust the bottle at Susan. She swatted his arm aside and turned away in contempt, which made the two hunters roar with laughter. This went on for over twenty minutes. Catherine started to rise at one point but was gruffly ordered by Eb to stay right where she was.

Had Fargo still carried a gun, he would have picked the two men off then and there. As things stood, he was helpless to intervene. Neither the spear nor his improvised bow were reliable at such a range, and the toothpick was only good for close-up fighting.

Deep down, Fargo was extremely worried about the welfare of the women. This was the first night the two hunters were alone with them, and there was no telling what Justis and Eb might do. The whiskey the pair were downing didn't bode well at all.

Suddenly Eb and Susan got into a heated argument. Their upraised voices reached Fargo.

"—get in that wagon when I tell you to!" the hunter roared.

"Never!" Susan shouted back. "You might as well get it through your head that none of us will stand by and let you have your way! You'll have to kill us first."

"You think I won't?" Eb bellowed, his hand dropping to the Colt wedged under his belt. "Just you watch me, bitch!"

Justis grabbed his partner's wrist and said something that prompted Eb to reluctantly relax, but Eb repeatedly glared at Susan afterward.

Fargo's every instinct goaded him to action. Yet he could

think of no means of freeing the women without endangering them in the bargain. He considered sneaking around to the wagons to see if his Sharps or any other guns were stored inside, yet balked at the risk; the mules and horses might give him away. And if the hunters suspected he was in the vicinity, they just might hold a gun to the women and threaten to shoot if he didn't step into the open.

Other ideas suggested themselves. Fargo could wait until later when the women were in the wagons asleep and at least one of the hunters would also be slumbering, then creep in close and overpower whoever was standing guard. Again, the slightest noise, the snap of a twig, would forewarn the pair and spoil everything.

Or Fargo could attempt to lure the hunters from the circle of firelight by making noise or using the buffalo hide. The flaw there was that in all likelihood only one of the men would come to investigate, and if the one who stayed behind heard a commotion or a shot he might use the women as a screen or shoot one out of sheer outrage.

Ordinary outlaws would have been easier for Fargo to deal with than the buffalo hunters, simply because most outlaws, despite their mean streaks, treated women with a degree of respect. Justis and Eb, however, had already shown they had no reservations about killing women if they felt it necessary. They had to be treated differently.

Another flurry of sharp words drew Fargo's gaze to the activity around the fire. Eb had risen and seized Danette by the arm and was trying to drag her toward the south wagon. The rest of the women were in a furious uproar, all of them shouting at once. Justis jumped up and pointed his rifle at them.

"Shut up and stay still or else!"

Susan, ignoring him, rose. But she was not quite fully upright when he lashed out with his rifle, jabbing the barrel into her stomach and knocking her over backward.

"I warned you, damn it!" Justis thundered, and tucked his buffalo gun to his shoulder. "You'll serve as a lesson for the others."

Fargo had seen enough. He shot erect and was all set to dash into the open to draw Justis's attention from Susan when he saw Danette's arm flick out and her long fingernails rake Eb across the face, drawing blood. Eb howled and jerked back, releasing her, and the instant she was loose, she whirled and raced to the west.

Justis, on hearing Eb's cry, had turned. "Stop!" he barked, shaking his rifle in his rage. "I'm through goin' easy on you!"

Danette continued running. She shoved a mule aside, ducked under the rope, and sprinted madly for the cover of the cottonwoods, her dress swirling around her legs.

A rifle blasted, only it wasn't Justis who fired. Eb had taken a hasty bead and squeezed off his shot just as Danette reached the limit of the firelight. She stumbled forward as if kicked from behind, sprawled onto her hands and knees, then frantically scrambled into the shadows.

"I got her!" Eb shouted. "Did you see? I got her good!"

Fargo was already in motion, speeding to the south, swinging in a loop around the wagons so he could reach Danette swiftly. The women were making enough racket to drown out any noise he made; Audris and Rita appeared hysterical, Catherine was wailing for Danette, and Susan was heaping language on Eb that would have made most upstanding young women blush with shame to merely think about.

Eb was hurrying to the rope. He paused there to survey the brush and trees, put a hand to his mouth, and called out, "Get your ass on back here, sister, and I'll go easy on you! Make me come after you, though, and I'm liable to finish you off."

By this time Fargo was due south of the wagons, stealthily moving through the inky gloom, his ears pricked to detect the telltale sound of Danette's footsteps. She was hurt, disoriented. She should be stumbling around, but he heard no noise other than his own soft tread and the clamor in the camp.

Fargo halted behind a tree to see which way Eb would move. The buffalo hunter was outside the rope corral now and advancing cautiously, perhaps out of fear that Danette would bean him with a rock if she could. He'd drawn the Colt, Fargo's Colt, and had cocked it.

"Speak to me, woman! You're only makin' me madder by doin' this."

There was no response, nor did Fargo expect one. Bent at the middle, he swung toward the stream to reduce the odds of Eb spotting him.

Back at the camp, Justis's voice rose shrilly above all the others: "That's enough! The next one of you who opens her mouth is dead!"

The man sure did like to make threats, Fargo reflected. He came to the grassy stretch bordering the water and stopped to get his bearings. To the northwest clumped Eb, barging through the undergrowth like an irate steer. Justis was having the women climb into one of the wagons at gunpoint. As yet, there was no trace of Danette.

Fargo sank to one knee, doing as the Indians did when they wanted to distinguish details at night. Objects higher than his head were now silhouetted against the dark blue background of the sky; movement would be easier to detect. But still Danette failed to appear. A chilling thought urged him forward: What if she was dead? She'd moved after she was shot, but she might be lying out there somewhere, either gone or bleeding to death.

"Where the hell are you?" Eb demanded from a spot twenty yards off.

Fargo's right hand closed on the hilt of the Arkansas toothpick and he slipped the knife out. Taking measured strides, he angled to intercept Eb. He'd delayed long enough, and his indecision had cost Danette dearly. First he'd slay Eb, then finish off Justis. Once the two hunters were disposed of, the women could help search for Danette.

"Eb?" Justis unexpectedly called. "Forget her and get back here."

"You want me to just leave her out here for the varmints to feed on?"

"All the trouble she gave us, I don't rightly care whether she lives or dies. You did the right thing shootin' her. We've still got the other four to sell and we'll make a heap of money off of them. We don't need that nag."

"All right. Whatever you say."

Fargo saw Eb begin to retrace his steps. The toothpick at his waist, he went faster to cut the hunter off. But he only took three paces when his right boot bumped a vague form slumped over in the grass, and at the contact the form voiced a wavering groan.

10

"I heard that!" Eb blurted, pivoting so fast he nearly tripped over his own feet. "Was that you? Come on out!"

Fargo had gone rigid at the sound, his boot touching Danette. Eb was looking directly at him, but from that far off the outline of Fargo's body blended into the brush and he was virtually invisible. Or so he hoped. He worked the knife around in his hand, palming the blade for a throw should Eb move closer.

"I heard you, woman!" Eb repeated, swaying slightly. "Step into the open and don't dawdle, neither. I give you my word I won't shoot you again."

Now there was a generous offer! Fargo thought to himself. The pressure on his boot suddenly shifted as Danette moved. To forestall another groan, Fargo took a chance and sank slowly down, his left hand groping over her body. He touched her back and felt a damp, sticky sensation. Blood. A lot of it. She moved again and his hand found her face. His palm gently covered her mouth as her lips parted. Thankfully, she made no sound.

"If this is the way you want it, fine," Eb declared angrily. "Lie out here and let the coyotes eat your innards. Serves you right. I sure as hell don't give a hoot." He headed for the wagons, the whiskey in his system making his gait unsteady.

Fargo didn't try to stop him. There was a more important problem to deal with now. He slid the toothpick into its sheath, then gently hooked his arms under Danette and lifted. She was lighter than she looked, no problem at all to carry back along the stream to his hiding place at the base of the bush. As he laid her down, she groaned again and her eyelids fluttered.

"What—?"

"Don't talk," Fargo cautioned. "You're safe, but I don't

know how badly you're hurt. I'll have to get under your dress to see."

Danette mumbled a few words, then slumped to one side, her hair framing her pale face like a halo.

Working rapidly, Fargo unbuttoned her dress and peeled the soaked fabric down until he found the wound. She had been extremely lucky. Eb's bullet had caught her high on the left side of her back, penetrating the fleshy area below her arm, and passed clean on through. No bones were broken, no vital organs had been hit. She'd lost a lot of blood initially but the flow had slackened a great deal. With some care, she'd be fine in a few days.

Fargo took the dress completely off to wash it. He was doubly glad he'd brought the buffalo hide along since it served to keep her warm while he took the garment to the stream. As he dipped it repeatedly in the water, he pondered his next move. Then, taking the meat and the dress, he ran a hundred yards farther downstream and placed both in the shelter of a thicket. Returning, he bore Danette to this new hiding place and made her as comfortable as he could.

The thicket hid the small fire he built in a hollow he scooped out of the earth with a stick. Using twigs and dry grass, he kept the flames low. It took a minute to find a pair of longer sticks on which he could impale pieces of buffalo meat. These sticks he jammed into the earth, slanted so that the meat was directly over the blaze. While their meal cooked, he hurried to the stream and filled his hat with water.

Danette had not stirred when he knelt by her side and dipped his right hand in the hat. He sprinkled water lightly over her face and neck, admiring the beauty of her smooth features and the red oval of her lips. Parting the hide, he drew his knife and cut off a strip from the bottom of her underdress. This he moistened and applied lightly to the wound to clean off the blood.

"That stings, handsome."

Fargo glanced up to see her regarding him with a strange expression. "If that bullet had been a few inches to the right, you wouldn't be feeling anything right now."

"Where is that bastard, anyway? Did you kill him?"

"Not yet, but I will. He's over at the wagons."

"Where did you come from?"

Fargo gave her a brief recital of all that had befallen him since they were separated, concluding with, "There's nothing I can do for the others for the time being."

"We never figured to see you again," Danette said softly. "Justis claimed he'd winged you and that you'd probably bled to death."

"Justis will be getting his soon, too." Fargo finished wiping her back and side and set the strip down. He raised his hat and held it close to her mouth, saying, "Take some. You'll need a lot of it if you're to get back on your feet quickly."

Danette lifted her head as he tilted the hat. She drank greedily, then sank back with a sigh. "Thank you." Her nose flared and she sniffed loudly. "This hide of yours stinks to high heaven. I'll smell like a slaughterhouse by morning."

"Keep it wrapped around you anyway," Fargo directed. "You need to stay warm until we're sure you don't have an infection." He pressed a palm to her forehead. As yet there was no evidence of a fever, but they wouldn't know for certain for a few more hours.

"You surprise me," Danette said.

"I surprise myself sometimes."

Danette smiled, displaying a row of fine white teeth. "I'm serious. You're not what we'd expected at all." Her smile widened. "We thought you'd be more like Justis and Eb."

"Sorry to disappoint you," Fargo said, shifting to check on the meat. The tantalizing aroma made his stomach growl.

"You can have both of those pieces," Danette offered. "I'm not hungry."

"You're having some," Fargo informed her. "You need to have food in your belly to keep up your strength and heal properly." He refrained from pointing out that more people died of infection from gunshot wounds than were killed outright in gunfights, and if she didn't stay nourished she'd be more susceptible to having infection set in. If that happened, her prospects for survival were exceedingly slim.

The wind had picked up and was rustling the trees and the grass. Raucous laughter wafted to their ears.

"Those two are animals!" Danette declared harshly. "You should have heard the way they were talking to us, the suggestions they made. If I was a church-going lady, I would have been shamed to tears."

"You're not?" Fargo asked absently, his attention on the sizzling meat.

"No," Danette said in a whisper. "But I will be once I have my husband. This is my big chance for a brand new start in life and I'm not about to do anything that will spoil it. I'm going to become the most God-fearing, upright woman anyone has ever known."

Fargo looked at her. "Is that what you want?"

"You bet your—," Danette began, and caught herself. "Yes, indeed," she went on demurely. "All of us feel the same way. We all want to begin over and do it right this time." Her eyes acquired a wistful aspect. "No one knows us out here. In Mountain City we'll be respectable, with homes of our own and men who really care for us. No more scraping by to make ends meet. No more doing what we don't want to do."

"No more Tom Orland?"

"Exactly," Danette said.

"What is his connection with you ladies? No one has bothered to explain it to me."

"You'll have to ask Susan about that."

"Why can't you tell me?"

"Because," Danette said. Her mouth scrunched up and she studied him thoughtfully for a moment. "This isn't fair. After all you've done for us, I figure you have a right to know the truth. But so help me, Fargo, I can't break my promise."

"Promise?"

"We all gave our word not to tell a soul about the reason we're heading west. We vowed never to talk about our past, no matter what." Danette paused. "It was Susan's idea."

Fargo plucked a stick from the ground, touched a finger to the meat, then licked off the savory grease and commented, "Hot and ready." He gave her the other morsel and settled down to partake of his meal.

"You're not going to ask me any more about our little secret?" Danette inquired, sounding surprised.

"No." Fargo took a bite and closed his eyes, relishing the taste of the first real food he'd had in almost two days. He was so hungry he could have eaten the whole buffalo and still had room for fresh apple pie.

"You sure are a puzzle," Danette said. "Most men would be trying to worm the truth out of me right about now."

Fargo interrupted his eating long enough to respond, "You made a promise to the others, didn't you? I happen to believe that when a person gives their word, they should keep it." He wagged his stick at her. "Now shut up and let me finish this in peace."

Shock was Danette's first reaction, then she laughed lightly and attended to her meat, her eyes on him whenever she thought he wouldn't notice.

But Fargo did. As he ate, he reviewed all that had happened since he'd met the women and recalled some comments they had made. Everything led to an obvious conclusion, but he kept his hunch to himself. If they wanted to tell him, they were welcome to. Otherwise, he'd respect their privacy.

The juicy steak only whetted Fargo's appetite. He broke the stick into pieces to feed to the fire, then sat back with his hands propped behind him and listened to distant off-key singing. From the sound of things, the buffalo hunters had about polished off their whiskey, and he wondered if they were so drunk they'd pass out. Most likely they wouldn't, not in light of the notorious capacity of their rowdy breed for drinking alcohol as if it were water.

Fargo looked at Danette to see if she was done and grinned on finding her asleep, her half-eaten meat lying on her chest. He took it off and folded the hide tighter around her to ward off the chill night air. In the dancing glow of the fire she was incredibly lovely, and he envied the man she was going to marry.

Lying back, Fargo put his hands behind his head and gazed at the multitude of stars dotting the heavens. His life sure did take some peculiar turns sometimes. Here he was, risking his skin to save a bunch of women who viewed him as some kind of ogre. If he'd had any common sense, he wouldn't have become mixed up with them in the first place. But that had always been his weakness. He never could resist a pretty face, even when he knew it involved trouble with a capital *T*. One day, he mused, his weakness might be the death of him.

In due course Fargo fell asleep, to be awakened some time later when Danette rolled over and wound up flush against his side. He let her sleep, draping an arm around her protectively before he closed his eyes again. When next he opened them, she was already awake and staring at him quizzically. Beyond her the eastern sky contained vivid streaks of pink and yellow. "Morning," he said. "How do you feel?"

"Sore, but better." Danette made no attempt to move. "Thanks to you. If you hadn't found me, I shudder to think what would have happened."

"Any fever?" Fargo asked, his hand going to her brow again. There was none, and his relieved smile brought an answering one from her. "You stay put. I have to go check on your friends." Lifting his arm from her shoulders, he stood and gathered up his spear, bow, and arrows.

"You be careful, Skye Fargo. I don't want those vermin to get you."

"Makes two of us," Fargo said. Stooping, he dashed through the thicket and along the stream, hoping to reach the camp while one of the buffalo hunters was still asleep. If the man on guard should be dozing, he'd have Danette snug in a wagon before sunrise.

Fargo hadn't covered twenty yards when he heard the yells of Justis and Eb as the pair urged the women to get the wagons moving, followed seconds later by the rattle of the Conestogas. He fell flat in the high grass, his lips tight as he watched the procession emerge from the cottonwoods and cross the stream, bearing south. One of the wheels on the last wagon wobbled a bit, as if it were loose or the spokes had been weakened.

Frustration just kept piling on top of frustration. With all the carousing the pair had done during the night, Fargo had counted on them getting a late start. They must be in a God-awful hurry to reach the Comancheros and sell the women if they were up and moving before daylight. Damn them.

His Ovaro was tied to the rear Conestoga once more. The saddle had been stripped off and must be in the wagon.

Fargo waited until the white tops were mere dots before he stood and walked back to the thicket. He'd have to stay there for at least a day to give Danette time to recover, making it that much harder to overtake the buffalo hunters once he resumed the chase. Even worse, the farther south they traveled, the closer they'd get to Comanche country.

Danette was sitting up when he showed. "I heard them leave. What do we do?"

"We wait until you're fit enough to walk."

"I can walk now," Danette said and, grimacing, she tried to rise. But she barely got to her knees when a wave of weakness struck her and, uttering a gasp, she pitched forward.

Fargo was right there to catch her. "You darn fool," he muttered. "Keep this up and you'll make your wound worse. Then we'll be stuck here for days." He carefully lowered her to the grass and brushed a wisp of hair from her cheek.

"Sorry. I guess I'm not as strong as I thought."

"You're doing fine," Fargo said. "Better than most." And he meant it. Many women, and most men, would be whining or groaning in pain, too stricken to move, let alone stand. She was a scrapper, this Danette, and he liked her immensely. "I'll go see about rustling us up some breakfast. You take this." He gave her the toothpick so she'd have something she could use to protect herself.

Danette surveyed the sprawling plain. "Tell me the truth. Are we in all that much danger from Indians?"

"Some. If the Cheyennes find us, it all depends on what kind of mood they're in whether they try to take our hair or not. The Sioux sometimes come this far south, but I'm friendly with them." Fargo took an arrow and notched it to the string. With the bow in his right hand and the spear in his left, he started to walk off.

"Skye?"

The Trailsman stopped and glanced back.

"Those two bastards kept talking about how rich they'd be after they sold us to the Comancheros. If I remember correctly, aren't the Comancheros found down Texas way?"

"They are."

"Then it'll take weeks for Justis and Eb to get there."

"True."

"Good."

"Good?"

Danette nodded. "It gives us plenty of time to catch them. Once we do, I want to tie them down and roast their oysters over an open fire."

Chuckling, Fargo departed. He hiked along the ribbon of a stream, seeking small game. Sparrows flitted about in the trees. Twice he saw squirrels that wisely stayed high up, out of reach. Finally a black-tailed jackrabbit ran from behind a bush almost at his feet and bounded fifteen feet to the

107

edge of the buffalo grass. There, as its kind often did when fleeing from a predator, it stopped to look around and see if it was being pursued.

Fargo was ready. As an experienced frontiersman, he was intimately familiar with the habits and quirks of every animal found from the Mississippi to the Pacific. So when the jackrabbit stopped, he had already dropped the spear, raised the bow, and pulled the string back to his cheek. He sighted along the shaft, one of those he had extracted from the dead bull, and relaxed his fingers.

There was a blurred streak, and the barbed tip tore into the jackrabbit's throat, the impact flipping it over. Thrashing and convulsing, the rabbit rolled around on the ground for a full minute before venting a piercing squeal as death claimed it.

His stomach rumbling again, Fargo retrieved his prize and carried the jackrabbit by its huge hind legs back to their hideaway.

Danette took one look and frowned. "The poor little bunny."

"Would you rather starve?"

"Hell, no. I like rabbit as much as the next person."

Fargo took his knife and did the skinning. Since they were well sheltered, he added fuel to the fire until the blaze was twice as big as before. Finding two long sticks, he roasted the rabbit meat as he had the buffalo steaks.

"You are a handy gent to have around in a pinch," Danette commented once they were both chewing lustily.

Fargo saw her eyes appraising him and grinned. "You'd like it," he declared.

"Like what?"

"Making love to me."

Danette's mouth dropped open and the piece of rabbit she had just bitten off her stick fell out. "How dare you!" she exclaimed. "And just when I was beginning to think you were fairly decent, even if you are a man!" She shook the stick at him. "What gives you the wild notion I was thinking about making love to you?"

"Tell me you weren't."

"I—," Danette began, and suddenly flushed scarlet from her chin to her forehead. Aware that Fargo was right, she sputtered and finished with, "Never in a million years, mister! You have a swelled head if you believe differently."

"You can be honest," Fargo said casually as he nibbled. "I'm not about to jump you, if that's what's worrying you. I won't do a thing until you make the first move."

"Of all the gall!" Danette huffed, her face darkening even more. "Why is it all men feel that every woman who lays eyes on them can't wait to get them in bed?"

"I can't speak for all men," Fargo answered, "but I know when a woman is interested in me." He bit into the meat, then talked with his mouth full. "You tell me something. Why is it most women won't admit it when they want a man, even to themselves? Why are women afraid of the truth?"

"I'm not afraid of anything!" Danette retorted. "Especially men! You're all a bunch of animals, as far as I'm concerned."

"Even the man waiting for you in Mountain City?"

Embarrassment was replaced by anger as Danette clenched a small fist and glared at him. "Don't let me hear you mention him again. He's a saint compared to the likes of you. Angus has agreed to marry me, sight unseen. He doesn't care what I look like. He loves me as a person, not for my body."

"Can you really love a person you only know through letters?" Fargo wondered aloud.

"Of course. Some people are better at expressing their feelings on paper than they are in person. They can say the things they wouldn't dare voice otherwise."

"You don't strike me as the sort who ever has trouble expressing her feelings," Fargo mentioned. "Matter of fact, if anything, I suspect you don't always know when to keep quiet. That mouth of yours must get you in hot water quite a lot."

Danette seemed puzzled. "I'm not saying you're right and I'm not saying you're wrong." She paused. "But where did you learn to read people so well?"

"Reading sign is what I do best."

"Well, do me a favor and keep your comments about lovemaking to yourself. I certainly don't want to make love to you and I never, ever will."

A shrug was Fargo's response.

"You don't believe me?"

"I've decided to keep my comments to myself," Fargo mimicked her, and laughed with delight at the fury etching her fine features. "That's another thing. Why is it that women can't stand to have anyone get the better of them?"

"I suppose men can?"

Their argument a draw, they finished their breakfast in mutual silence. Fargo deliberately paid no attention whatsoever to Danette. He buried the parts of the jackrabbit they hadn't eaten, added a few branches to the fire, gathered more to use later, and then washed his face and hands in the stream. Filling his hat, he took it to her.

Danette accepted the water without saying a word.

"You need to clean the wound every so often," Fargo advised.

"I'm not about to let a lecher like you see me at my toilet," Danette responded stiffly. "A lady needs her privacy."

Sighing, Fargo picked up his spear. "Fine. I'll go for a walk."

"Go play in a buffalo herd, why don't you?"

The sun was well up, the day already hot. Fargo, for lack of anything better to do, walked to where the wagons had been parked. He found the empty whiskey bottle lying by the fire and stuck it in his pocket. The cork was nearby. To the north lay an overturned pot, perhaps tossed there by one of the buffalo hunters during the height of their revelry. This he added to his growing collection of odds and ends.

Fargo was walking in circles, searching for whatever else might have been carelessly discarded, when he heard a horse nicker off to the northeast. Doubling over, he sprinted into the cottonwoods on that side of the clearing, his pulse quickening at the thought of what he would see once the brush no longer blocked his view. He dropped to his knees and scooted the last few yards, stopping behind a trunk.

There they were.

A band of Indians, heading straight for the stream.

11

The five warriors were strung out in single file, a customary practice when on a raid in enemy territory. All five were painted for war, as were their horses. None had guns, but three held ash bows and the others carried glittering lances. The style of their hair and their buckskins identified them not as Cheyenne or Sioux, but as Kiowas, and the Kiowas were as bloodthirsty as the Comanches where whites were concerned.

Fargo flattened himself on the ground and set the pot aside. The five would reach the stream at a point halfway between his position and the thicket in which Danette was concealed. He hoped they would water their mounts and keep going, but he was doomed to be disappointed.

Suddenly one of the braves cried out and pointed at the ground to his left. To a man they gathered around, talking excitedly.

Fargo knew the reason and sorely wished he had a gun. The Kiowas had spied the tracks made by the Conestogas. Wagons meant white men, and no self-respecting Kiowa ever passed up the opportunity to take a white scalp.

Abruptly fanning out, the Kiowas rode toward the cottonwoods, their weapons held ready for use.

Fargo dared not try to scramble into deeper cover. They'd spot him the moment he did. His only recourse was to lie there as flat as a flapjack and rely on the grass and brush to hide him from their prying eyes. The wind, thankfully, was blowing from due north to due south, so his scent wouldn't be detected by the war ponies.

One of the warriors, the tallest of the bunch, appeared to be the leader. At gestures from him, two of the others cut off to one side to approach the cottonwoods from another angle. A third man swung toward the stream to come up on the campsite from that direction.

Fargo felt his mouth go completely dry as the pair to the east neared his hiding place. If they saw him, he'd be in for the scrape of his life. Armed as he was with just the spear and his knife, he might be able to drop one or two, but the rest would assuredly get him. If he'd brought the bow he might be able to give a better account of himself, yet in the end the outcome would be the same.

Only one of the braves was making straight for the very spot where Fargo was lying. The other was a bit to the right. Fargo concentrated on the Indian who posed the greatest threat. The warrior rode alertly, a part of his animal, his posture showing he was primed to let fly with an arrow at a heartbeat's notice.

Many times Fargo had seen warriors loose shafts so swiftly the human eye could not follow their motions, and he had no desire to learn if this particular brave was equally skilled. He peered through the tiny branches of a low bush that flanked the tree, waiting for any sign that he had been seen. The Kiowa was scanning the trees behind him and to either side.

Fargo saw the war pony's eyes swivel toward the base of his tree and he braced for the worst, but the animal gave no indication it had spied him. A moment later the warrior slanted to the left to enter a gap in the cottonwoods. Fargo stayed motionless until the thud of hoofs told him both of the Kiowas had gone by, then he twisted and silently rose into a crouch.

All five warriors were converging on the spot where the fire had been. Convinced their quarry was gone, they began talking again. A debate took place, with four of the braves evidently wanting to go after the wagons and the fifth, for some reason, not caring to. At last the tall Kiowa moved his mount up next to the dissenter's and lashed the man across the cheek with his quirt.

What might have happened next no one would ever know, because at that very instant a shout carried loud and clear from downstream.

"Fargo? I'm done. Where are you?"

The Trailsman suppressed an urge to curse a blue streak. He saw the Kiowas snap around, then whisper urgently as they spread out once again. In a ragged line they moved into the cottonwoods, heading for Danette. They would pass to the left of him, within a few yards at most.

"Fargo?"

Damn, dumb female! Fargo silently fumed, and gripped the spear firmly as he edged to one side, up behind a wider tree closer to the Kiowas. None were bothering to scan the brush nearest to them; they had their heads tilted back or cocked to listen for another shout so they could pinpoint exactly where it came from. Fargo dug in his boot heels, coiled his legs, and when the closest was only six feet away, he darted around the trunk and drove the spear up and in.

Caught unawares, the Kiowa glanced down just as the charred point ripped into his stomach. A screech tore from his throat as he was yanked from his mount and slammed to the hard ground.

Fargo's leg snapped out, his boot catching the warrior on the chin. With a savage wrench he jerked the spear out, then whirled and leaped astride the startled war horse. The other Kiowas had either stopped or wheeled their mounts at the fifth man's wail, and now two of them dug their heels into their horses and charged.

Hemmed in by the trees and the brush, Fargo was at a disadvantage. They could close in from several sides at once, trapping him. To gain room to maneuver, he goaded the war horse into a gallop and ducked low a fraction of a second before an arrow cleaved the very space his head had just occupied. Skirting several trees, he broke into the open and turned to the right, toward the stream.

Yipping in rage, the Kiowas were hard on his heels.

Another shaft almost clipped Fargo's shoulder. He came to the water and changed course yet again, sliding onto the off-side of the horse as he did, causing the warriors to hold their fire until they had a better target. Dangling close to the horse's flying hoofs, he desperately tried to think of a way to come out of the fight alive.

Two of the four Kiowas were angling to the left so they could get a clear shot at him while the last two were racing like madmen to overhaul him from the rear.

So many times in the past had Fargo's life depended on split-second decisions that they came as second nature to him. In this instance, at the very moment he realized he must do something totally unexpected to confuse the warriors if he wanted to live, he did it. Pulling himself up, but staying bent over the horse's neck, he tugged on the reins and brought the animal to a sliding stop. So unexpected was this development that three of the Kiowas swept past him before they could react.

The fourth brave was a shade slower and closer than his fellows. He drew alongside Fargo and hoisted his lance high, but Fargo was faster and had his own spear swinging in an arc that ended in the brave's chest. The man toppled. As he did, Fargo let go of his crude spear and tugged the lance from the dying warrior's grasp.

One of the other Kiowas had managed to rein up and turn. Now he adjusted his arrow on his sinew string and in the same motion extended his bow.

The range was a mere ten feet. Fargo was by no means an expert with a lance but he could throw one well enough to hit a man at that distance. Shifting, he flashed his right arm in an overhand throw, and was rewarded for his effort by seeing the lance transfix the bowman's throat.

The next second, Fargo had hauled on the reins to turn the horse around and was in full flight down the stream. Strident whoops confirmed the last two warriors were in pursuit. One had a bow, the other a lance. It was the former Fargo rated as the greater threat, the man he watched. He saw the brave take aim and resorted again to the Sioux trick of hanging from the side of his mount.

This time, however, the Kiowa was too enraged to hold his fire. Quite the opposite. He intentionally aimed at the animal and loosed his shaft.

Fargo felt the horse shudder when it was hit and heard its piercing whinny. He saw its legs start to buckle. Pushing off before it could crash down on top of him, he landed on his shoulders, jolting his spine, and rolled end over end until he smacked into a tree. Dazed but unwilling to lie there and be killed, he shoved off the ground with his left arm as his right hand gripped the Arkansas toothpick.

The Kiowas thought he was defenseless. The bowman had slowed and was nocking another arrow while bearing down in a beeline.

Rattled though Fargo was, he had the presence of mind to snake out his throwing knife, heft it once for balance, and fling it with all the power in his broad shoulders and upper arm. The blade sparkled in the sunlight as it crossed the intervening space. The thud of the knife sinking into the warrior's body was drowned out by the drumming of hoofs. Not so the yell the Kiowa gave before pitching over backward.

Fargo didn't squat there to watch the man fall. Jumping up, he spun and dashed into the trees, the sound of the last brave's mount like thunder in his ears. He glanced back just as the Kiowa threw his lance, and the act accidentally saved his life. The lance missed his head by the slimmest of margins, coming so close it brushed his hair. Fargo began to wheel to confront the warrior and neglected to keep an eye on the ground. His right boot hit something. He tripped.

The last of the war party sounded like a screaming cougar as he drew a big knife and launched himself from the back of his horse.

Fargo was in the act of rising. He only got to his elbows when the warrior rammed into him. All the breath in his lungs whooshed out. Overwhelming pain coursed through his body from head to toe. Stunned, he realized the Kiowa was straddling his chest and looked up to see the brave elevating the knife. He tried to bring his arm up to deflect the blow but his muscles wouldn't cooperate.

"No, damn you!"

From out of the blue a long length of tree limb whizzed, striking the Kiowa on the ear. The Indian sagged, then snarled and twisted, trying to evade another swing. But he was struck full on the mouth. His lips split and blood spurted. He hurled himself to the left and scrambled to his feet.

Fargo could see Danette preparing to strike again. The exertion had weakened her, though, and she was gritting her teeth from the strain. She needed help, which he gave by drawing his right leg back and kicking the Kiowa in the knee. There was a loud crunch and the warrior stiffened, then fell forward. Fargo brought up his own knee, smashing the brave in the nose. The man fell right beside him.

Rolling, Fargo seized the Kiowa's wrist to hold the knife at bay and pounded his knee into the warrior's stomach twice in swift succession. The brave doubled over, momentarily weakened, enabling Fargo to clamp both of his hands on the hand holding the knife and bend the arm backward. Then, with a violent thrust, Fargo buried the blade at the base of the Kiowa's chin and held on tight while the warrior shook and blubbered and fought fiercely to free himself. At length the Indian's struggles grew weaker and finally he sagged limply to the grass.

"You did it!" Danette said, sinking down and resting a hand on Skye's arm.

"No thanks to you," Fargo snapped, lying back to catch his breath. His blood was pounding through his veins, his temples were throbbing. He could hardly believe he had slain all five Kiowas in the span of two or three minutes, yet that was exactly what had happened. Looking down, he took stock, amazed to find he was unhurt.

"What's bothering you?" Danette asked. "I came to help once I saw them after you, didn't I?"

Fargo sat up, his nose almost touching hers. "They wouldn't have been after me in the first place if you had the brains of a sage hen! What possessed you to yell like you did?"

Danette stared at the dead Kiowa. "Oh. That. I was lonely and wanted some company. I didn't think there would be any harm in calling out to you."

"Next time do it louder so the Comanches will hear you clear down in Texas," Fargo said bitterly.

"You told me there wasn't that much danger from Indians," Danette said defensively. "How was I to know there would be Cheyennes so close?"

"These are Kiowas," Fargo informed her, drawing his legs up under him and slowly standing. A kink in his back made him wince.

"Kiowas? You never mentioned a word about any damn Kiowas! It seems to me you should have made things a lot clearer than you did."

Fargo made a motion of disgust and walked toward the last brave's horse, which was standing ten feet away, waiting for its master. "Whoa there, boy," he said softly, relying on his quiet voice and gentle bearing to calm the animal so he could get closer. "There's nothing to be afraid of." The war horse bobbed its head but made no attempt to flee. Moving at a snail's pace so as not to alarm it, he placed his hand on the reins and stroked its neck.

Danette had not moved. She couldn't seem to tear her gaze from the warrior. "I never saw a man killed before," she remarked.

"Happens all the time out here," Fargo said. "You'd better get used to it if you plan to live in the West." He tethered the horse to a limb, then walked to the stream to find the other animals. Two of them were drinking not far off. One shied at his approach but didn't run away, and he soon had both in hand and was leading them toward the thicket.

Danette fell into step at his side. "Would it help any if I say I'm sorry?"

"It would be a start."

"You're a spiteful man, Skye Fargo. Do you know that?"

"Why? Because I like living?" Fargo countered, and she clamped her mouth shut. He secured the horses, then brought over the other one. The animal that had been hit with the arrow was dead of a punctured lung, blood dribbling from its nostrils, while the fifth horse had disappeared and was probably on its way back to Kiowa territory.

Fargo dragged the bodies that were near the stream away from it so the corpses wouldn't contaminate the water as they decomposed. Gathering up the fallen weapons, he trudged wearily into the thicket and set them down in a pile near the fire.

Danette was huddled in the shadows, her head bowed, her face masked by her hair.

A twinge of guilt assailed the Trailsman and he stepped around the flames to kneel in front of her. "Look," he began in a kinder tone than he felt like using, "I can't be acting like your nursemaid every minute of the day. You have to use some common sense and not do anything that might get us both killed." He paused, waiting for her to speak, and when she didn't, he went on. "I do appreciate your coming to help me. It took a lot of gumption, and it couldn't have been easy with you in pain like you are. So why don't we make up and be friends again, unless you'd rather—."

Danette's head snapped up, revealing streaks of moisture lining her cheeks. Uttering a low moan, she threw herself at him and wrapped her arms around his.

"What—?" Fargo said in surprise, and had the rest of his question smothered by her soft lips as they clamped onto his mouth. Her velvet tongue darted out to caress his. Her nails dug into his shoulders. He was too dumbfounded to do more than half-heartedly respond to her kiss, and when she broke it and smiled at him he shook his head in amazement. "What the hell was that for?"

"Don't tell me the great Trailsman is complaining. Sue told me you're always ready and willing."

"How would she know?" Fargo responded.

"She met—," Danette started to answer, but changed her mind and said instead, "What does it matter? All that counts is I want you." Her hands roved over his chest and down to his flat abdomen. "God, you're muscled like a bull!"

"What about me being a lecher?"

"You were right all along. I did want you. I've wanted you since the first time I laid eyes on you in Abilene," Danette disclosed, lowering her moist lips to his throat.

"And what about your wound? I don't want you to start bleeding again."

"Then be gentle," Danette said, giggling. Her tongue lathered his neck, trailing steadily lower. Her hands had found his organ.

Fargo was over his initial surprise. Her touch was having the desired effect, stirring his manhood and fanning his lust to a fever pitch. And while he was bewildered by her drastic change in attitude, he had never been one to look the proverbial gift horse in the mouth. "You pick the damnedest time," he growled, and cupped her twin mounds.

A tremulous "Ohhhhhhhh!" fluttered from Danette's rosy lips. She arched her back, sighing, "It's been so long!"

The passionate statement jarred Fargo's memory. He recalled Catherine using the exact same words a few nights back. It confirmed his earlier hunch, and he came close to laughing aloud at the thought of five sex-starved women hiring *him* to escort them across the Plains. Having a fox guard a henhouse would make just as much sense.

Danette had hooked her mouth to his right ear and seemed to be striving to chew it off.

Fargo gave her breasts a hard squeeze, eliciting a hungry moan. His mouth found hers again and this time his tongue did the probing. She squirmed against him, grinding her hips into his loins, which brought his hands down to her buttocks. He wanted to stay away from her shoulders and back anyway, since he really feared opening her wound. Sticking a finger between her thighs, he stroked back and forth, feeling the friction heighten the heat in her body.

"I want you so bad," Danette said.

Fargo slowly eased backward until he was lying down. Never losing his grip on her, he circled her small waist with his big hands and lifted her small frame, placing her down so that she was straddling him. This way her wound would be spared the pressure of bearing his weight. His hands rubbed up and down her willowy legs, molding her soft thighs like a sculptor molded clay.

"Damn, you're good."

"You haven't seen nothing yet," Fargo promised, hoisting her dress high enough for his right hand to slip underneath. Her thighs were silken; they quivered as he massaged them. He worked his way to the bushy triangle above, stuck a finger inside her undergarments, and found her slit. At the contact she bucked, her hands clamping onto the front of his shirt for support.

"Ah! Ah!" Danette cried.

Fargo added another finger and plunged both into her womanhood. He expected her to catch fire, but he wasn't prepared for the frenzy of pumping and thrusting that nearly broke his fingers. Her limpid eyes were hooded, her mouth slack, and she grunted each time her hips came down. If her wound was bothering her, it didn't show or slow her in the slightest. She was lost in a world of her own, oblivious to all else save the exquisite sensations coming from her core.

Content to let her enjoy herself, Fargo did little but work on one of her breasts as he stroked faster and faster. Danette panted now, and her lips trembled. She was on the very brink. To help her over the edge, Fargo abruptly grasped her from behind with his free hand and rammed his fingers into her slick tunnel as if he were trying to impale her on his arm.

"Oh, God! Yes! Yes! Don't stop!" Danette said. Then, urgently, as her body went into a paroxysm of ecstasy, "I'm coming! Like never before! I'm coming!"

The torrent that poured over Fargo's hand was proof. He held tight to increase her joy and let her pump herself out. When she groaned and sagged against him, he deftly hiked her dress higher, moved the last garment aside and, undoing his pants in record time, fed his pole into her.

"Sweet merciful heaven!" Danette exclaimed, her eyes as wide as walnuts. "I was right. You *are* a bull!"

Fargo put a firm hand on each slender hip and bucked

upward, raising her clear off the ground. Danette gasped, wriggled, voiced inarticulate sounds. He continued the bucking motion, pacing himself, in no rush to reach his peak. She slumped forward, too weak to stay upright any more.

The only sounds for the next few minutes were the thud of Fargo's rear end hitting the ground and the increasingly drawn-out moans issuing from Danette. They were glued at the waist, inseparable until the end. When it came, Fargo himself cried out and Danette rose, her mouth gaping in a silent scream of sheer delirium. Their bodies heaved and swayed in primeval rhythm. The explosion was earth-shaking, and both of them forgot her wound as they went wild in physical abandon.

Presently Fargo coasted to a stop and was still, his body bathed in perspiration, his heart thumping madly. Danette collapsed on top of him and her lips brushed his chin. "Are you all right?" he croaked.

"Never better," she answered contentedly. "I've found just the cure for gunshots."

They lay quietly for a long time. It was Fargo who stirred first, running his fingers through her hair and raising her head so he could see her face. "You're a lot tougher, lady, than I figured."

"Is that good?"

"You bet your ass it is. Now we can head out at first light tomorrow after your friends and those two buffalo-butchering sons of bitches."

"And then?"

"I have a big surprise in store for them."

12

They had been riding for two hours when Skye Fargo decided to stop for a short while in order for Danette to rest. She was holding up well but her back and shoulder were so sore and tender she couldn't bear to have either touched. Their lovemaking of the day before hadn't opened the wound, but it had caused the area around the wound to swell up.

Fargo held onto the reins of the two war horses they were riding and the one he had been leading because he didn't trust them not to run off if given the chance, and he didn't care to be left stranded afoot a second time. He pushed his hat back as he watched Danette sit down. So far her wound wasn't infected, but if the swelling became any worse, he might have to lance it with the toothpick to draw out any pus. Which reminded him. "I've been meaning to ask you," he commented. "How did you get your hands on my throwing knife? I thought Orland had taken it."

Danette grinned self-consciously. "I took it when we carried you to our wagon after you were pistol-whipped." She folded her arms across her waist and bent forward to ease the strain on her swollen back. "I know I shouldn't have, but when my hand bumped it I couldn't resist. When none of the others were looking, I slipped the thing under my dress." Her face turned southward. "I figured it would be the perfect ace in the hole if Orland got his grubby hands on us."

"Thanks for giving it back when you did."

"I knew you were our last hope," Danette said. She winked at him. "Plus I had taken quite a shine to you, and I didn't want you killed before I found out if all those stories Sue told had been true."

"I'll have to thank her for getting you so curious," Fargo said.

Five minutes later they were back on the trail, riding side by side. Danette glanced back at the third horse and asked, "I can understand why you brought the pot along, so we can cook our food. And I understand why you brought the whiskey bottle full of water, too. But for the life of me I don't see why you're dragging that stinking buffalo hide all over creation."

"Justis and Eb are buffalo hunters, aren't they?"

"Yes," Danette said. "But what does that have to do with anything?" She stared thoughtfully at the hide, then declared, "Oh!"

Fargo didn't expect to overtake the Conestogas before dark since they had a full day's lead, so he was mildly surprised and considerably puzzled when shortly after noon he spied the arched white canvas tops on the horizon. The wagons were right out in the open, nowhere near shelter or water, and he wondered why naturally cautious men like Justis and Eb would make such a blunder. Had something happened? More Kiowas, maybe?

"Come on," Fargo said, reining to the left so he could swing wide and study the situation. He stayed far enough out that the only way the hunters would spot him was if they climbed on top of the Conestogas to scour the countryside, an unlikely occurrence.

Danette was apprehensive. "What if those bastards got carried away? I swear, if one of my friends has been harmed, I'll use that knife of yours to turn both of those hairy apes into eunuchs."

Minutes later the ground sloped away before them and they found themselves in a dry wash littered with stones and broken limbs washed there from points west during heavy spring rains. Fargo swung down and tied the horses, then took a bow and quiver of arrows with him as he climbed back to the top.

"What's next?" Danette asked at his elbow.

"Watch the horses while I see what's going on."

"I want to go, too."

"You're going to crawl through the grass in your condition?" Fargo said, and left her standing there as he headed to the southwest. Crouching down, he jogged at a brisk clip until he was close enough to distinguish figures moving about near the wagons. He saw the mules and horses tethered south of them. Sinking onto his belly, Fargo crawled forward. Soon the reason the Conestogas had stopped became apparent.

One of the wheels had broken. The wagon had hit a rut, and the sudden shifting of weight had caused several spokes on the rear wheel on the left side to snap in half. Justis and Eb were working on the problem, using tools the women had wisely included for just such an emergency, but it was evident they were poor craftsmen and knew precious little about repairing busted wheels.

Fargo inched near enough to overhear snatches of conversation. He saw Sue approach the pair and regard them with open scorn.

"How many more weeks will this take?"

"Go to hell, missy!" Justis snapped.

"We've been here since late yesterday morning," Sue ignored him. "We don't have any fresh meat and we're low on water. What happens when we run out?"

"You'll be too weak to flap those gums of yours," Eb said, and both hunters cackled merrily.

"I'm serious, damn you," Sue said. "Why doesn't one of you take a water bag back to that stream and fill it up?"

Justis put down the mallet he held, then stood. "Oh, sure. You'd like that, wouldn't you? If one of us leaves, it'd be that much easier for you women to jump the one who stays." He shook his head. "No sirree, missy. We stick together always. And if you'll stop botherin' us every five minutes, we'll have this wheel set to go by sundown."

"If you don't stop botherin' us," Eb added ominously, "I might forget how much money you'll fetch from the Comancheros and do to you like I did to that uppity Danette."

In a huff Sue flounced off, over to where Catherine, Audris, and Rita stood by the other wagon. They talked in low tones, repeatedly glaring at their captors.

Fargo had heard enough. Backing off, he cautiously worked his way across the prairie to the dry wash and found Danette perched on the rim, anxiously awaiting him. She grabbed his arm as he started down the incline.

"Well? Don't keep me in suspense."

Briefly, Fargo told her all he had seen and heard, and while doing so he moved along the wash bed collecting the longest, straightest limbs he could find. Many were too dry and brittle to use, but he had found enough to make two piles when Danette's curiosity got the better of her.

123

"What exactly are you doing?"

Fargo patiently explained and smiled at the devilish light that animated her eyes. She joined in, and working together they soon had enough for his purpose. He drew his toothpick and trimmed some to the proper length. Next he took the buffalo hide off the spare horse and cut a half-dozen thin strips to be used in tying the branches together. Under his guidance, Danette assisted him in constructing the frame. He thought it was sturdy enough, but when they threw the hide over it, several of the uprights buckled. So they reinforced the weak sections and tried again. Then, using short strips, he tied up the corners and arranged the contours to his liking. At last he stepped back and studied their handiwork. "What do you think?"

Danette nodded in appreciation and laughed. "Trailsman, you're about as devious as they come. I'm glad you're on my side."

Well before sunrise the next morning everything was set up and Fargo was in position to see all that transpired. He was screened by the high grass, invisible from afar. His head came up when he observed Eb emerge from the second wagon and go over to the fire where Justis sat bundled in a heavy robe. Eb leaned down and poured himself a tin cup of coffee. As Eb straightened, he happened to gaze eastward, and he was so startled by what he saw that he upended some of the hot brew onto the front of his shirt and yelped. When Justis looked up, Eb pointed and jabbered, and Justis leaped erect.

Fargo firmed his grip on the end of the long strip of hide he had in his left hand. His right hand rested on the bow in front of him. An arrow lay across the bow, already notched. Beside the bow was a full quiver. He'd taken his throwing knife and wedged it under his belt on his right hip in case he should miss with his shafts. All had been done that could be done. Now it was up to the buffalo hunters. Would they mount up and give chase, or would they grab their rifles and shoot from there? He'd positioned the decoy seventy yards from the wagons during the dead of night, close enough for a skilled marksman, yet not so close that they could tell the decoy wasn't real.

Justis and Eb were doing exactly as the Trailsman

wanted; they were both taking aim. By both firing at once, they were hoping to drop their target right where it stood.

Fargo tensed his left arm. He had to be ready at the right instant or they might become suspicious. Eyes locked on their rifles, he waited until both guns boomed and belched smoke and lead, then he yanked as hard as he could on the hide rope. Ten yards away, the imitation buffalo he had put together with Danette's help toppled over on its side. So cleverly had he arranged the shape of the hide that, from a distance, the decoy closely resembled a young cow.

Yelps of delight came from the two hunters. The shots had awakened the women, and all four were climbing down from the first wagon.

Fargo released the hide and grasped the bow and arrow. He held his breath, waiting to see if both men or only one would come out to check the "dead" buffalo.

The pair were reloading. Once they had, Eb covered the women while Justis ran to his horse and mounted without bothering to saddle up. His legs flailing, he galloped toward the huge bundle of hide and branches. He was smirking, no doubt at the thought of a juicy steak for breakfast and all the jerky they could make to tide them over on the journey south to Comanchero country.

Lifting the bow a few inches, Fargo glanced toward the wagons. Eb wasn't paying much attention to his friend; he was bantering with the women. Which suited Fargo just fine. He swiveled, his gut tightening as Justis came closer and closer and finally reined up a dozen feet from the decoy.

"Got you!" Justis beamed, leaping down. He took only two strides when he realized something was amiss and stopped short. "What the hell?" he blurted.

Fargo had risen to his knees and pulled the bow string all the way back. Sighting along the shaft, he centered the point squarely on the hunter's head and said softly, "We meet again, stupid."

Justis whirled, his face lined in shock. Frantically he tried to level his rifle, but he had raised it only a few inches when there was a loud twang and the arrow materialized in the middle of his face as if by magic. Justis staggered rearward, his mouth working like that of a fish out of water. His knees gave way. He whined once, and pitched forward.

A shout of rage came from the Conestogas as Skye Fargo

shoved upright and raced to the fallen hunter. In the blink of an eye he had Justis's rifle in his hands and was whirling, the stock tucked to his shoulder, his thumb pulling back the hammer. He saw Eb doing the same, and he was not yet ready to fire when Eb did. A hornet stirred the air. Fargo responded in kind an instant later.

Eb behaved as if kicked by one of the mules. He flew backward, his arms out and flapping like the wings of a butterfly, and crashed into the last wagon. His rifle fell from his nerveless fingers. He tried to straighten but couldn't, then slumped to the ground.

It took only four strides for Fargo to reach Justis's mount and jump up. Grabbing the reins, he rode hard for the wagons, concerned Eb might only be wounded. But his haste proved to be unnecessary, as he confirmed when he galloped up and found Eb gaping lifelessly at the azure sky, a neat round hole in the center of the man's forehead.

"Fargo!" Sue cried, rushing up to him. The others were on her heels, and they all began talking at once, asking questions or praising his shooting.

"Quiet down!" Fargo ordered, holding aloft his hand to accent his command. Sliding off the horse, he walked over to Eb, bent down, and pulled his Colt from under the hunter's belt. He leaned Justis's rifle against the wagon so he could check the cylinder and verify it held five cartridges, then he twirled the Colt into his holster and turned around. "Where's my Sharps?"

"Your rifle?" Sue said. "In the wagon behind you. But where—?" she started to ask, and stopped.

Fargo had turned again and was walking to the front of the Conestoga. Gripping the seat, he pulled himself up and looked within. The Sharps was there, all right, propped against an open, empty water keg. He made sure it was loaded and was about to jump off when he spied his saddle at the back of the wagon. Hopping down, he walked around, reached in, and hauled the saddle and his saddle blanket out.

The women were noting his every action. There was no doubt they were perplexed by his urgency.

"Mr. Fargo?" Catherine began.

"Harness the mules and be ready to move out as soon as I get the wheel fixed, which shouldn't take more than an hour," Fargo interrupted her. "We're heading back to the stream so you can load up with water like you should have done before."

"We had other things on our minds," Sue responded, jerking a thumb at Eb. "Now tell us. What's your hurry?"

"I tangled with some Kiowas yesterday who might have been part of a bigger war party. If they were, and if the others are still in this area, they might have heard the shots," Fargo patiently explained. Going on, he was greeted with a nicker by the stallion. He stroked its neck a few times, then threw on the blanket and the saddle. As he secured the front cinch, Sue came up behind him.

"Where are you going?"

"I have a surprise for you." Fargo shoved the Sharps into the scabbard, hooked a boot in the stirrup, and swung up. To Sue's credit, she didn't badger him with more questions. He could have come right out and revealed he was eager to get back to Danette—whom he had left at the dry wash with a warning that if she didn't stay put he'd throw her over a knee and paddle the daylights out of her—but he didn't. Danette had said she couldn't wait to see their faces when she showed up, and he didn't intend to deprive her of her fun.

The Ovaro fairly flew to the wash. Fargo reined up in a spray of dust and uttered an oath: Danette and the two Indian ponies were gone! Riding to the bottom, he searched for tracks and found where the two horses had headed eastward along the wash floor. There was no rhyme or reason to it. Danette should have done as she'd been told and remained there where she was safe.

Concerned she would blunder into more Indians, Fargo galloped after her. Soon he came on fine dust particles hovering in the air, proof she wasn't far ahead. He went faster. Suddenly, rounding a bend, he saw her not fifteen feet away, coming directly toward him. In the barest nick of time he drew rein. The Ovaro had to swing aside to avoid a collision with the animal she was riding.

"Fargo!" Danette exclaimed happily.

"What the hell are you trying to do? Get yourself killed? I told you not to move, remember?"

"Ease up, handsome," Danette responded. With a bob of her head she indicated the spare horse, which she was leading. "This cayuse pulled loose and took off. I figured I should bring it back before it ran into some more of those Kiowas and they backtracked it to us."

"You did good," Fargo said, feeling a bit guilty about misjudging her. Taking the extra horse, he allowed Danette to assume the lead. She insisted on hearing all about his fight with the hunters and thanked him for not telling her friends that she was alive.

The astonishment and relief of the other women knew no bounds. Fargo busied himself with the wheel while the five of them hugged and kissed Danette, practically drowning her in their tears. He figured that was what Danette had been looking forward to all along.

It took over an hour, but Fargo got the wheel fixed and stored the tools. Now that they had additional horses, those women who wanted to could ride when it wasn't their turn to drive one of the wagons. Consequently, Susan Walker rode beside him as they retraced their steps to the stream.

"Danette told us all that you did for her," Sue mentioned when they were halfway there. "I can't thank you enough."

Fargo glanced at the Conestoga in which Danette was resting. "She's a tough little lady. She'll do her husband proud."

"We all will," Sue said, brushing at her raven hair. "You have no idea how much this means to us."

"I think I do."

Susan laughed. "You might think you do, but there's no way you could know. . . ."

"That you're all prostitutes?" Fargo finished, using the polite word so as not to offend her. "I've known that for some time."

Astonishment silenced Sue for long seconds. Finally she took a breath and said, "I shouldn't be surprised, but I am. What gave us away? Did you remember me?"

"You?"

"Yes. I was at a whorehouse in St. Louis a couple of years ago when you paid a visit. You picked one of the other girls even though I tried to catch your eye."

"My loss," Fargo grinned.

"No, it was mine. Bess didn't stop bragging about you for weeks." Sue studied his face. "If it wasn't me, how did you guess? We've worked so hard to cover our tracks and to come across as real ladies. Where did we go wrong?"

"Nowhere," Fargo assured her. "But like I told Danette,

reading sign is what I do best. I expect that's why folks call me the Trailsman." He chuckled. "It took me a while, but I was able to piece together enough to figure out that you're all tired of the trade and you want to start your lives over again in Mountain City."

"You don't know the half of it," Sue said, her tone melancholy. "We're desperate, Fargo. This marriage business might be the last chance any of us will ever have to become respectable." She sighed, her features downcast. "We had all reached the end of our rope. You've probably also guessed that we were working in one of Orland's houses when we decided to up and quit on him. He didn't take too kindly to that."

"Course not. He's afraid some of his other girls might get the same idea if he lets you get away with it. That's why he was waiting for you in Abilene."

Sue nodded. "He wants to take us back, whether we want to go or not," she said angrily. "Because of the contracts he made us sign when we first started working for him, he thinks he owns us lock, stock, and barrel."

"A pimp who makes his women work under a contract? That's a new one on me."

"It was new to us, too, but we liked the idea. Orland claimed we'd all be better off if everything was spelled out in black and white. But none of us bothered to read the fine print."

"What did it say?"

"That the only one who could cancel our contracts was Orland. We had to do whatever he wanted for as long as he wanted, and if we gave him a hard time he was entitled to take all of our earnings instead of the usual percentage."

Fargo remembered overhearing mention of a woman Orland knocked down some stairs. "He likes to beat his whores, too, doesn't he?"

"Yes." Sue sadly shook her head. "The slightest thing will set him off. He keeps a cane in his office, and he uses it every chance he gets."

"Maybe you'll be lucky and we'll run into him again."

"Why would that be lucky?"

"Because the next time we do, I aim to kill him."

Darkness had descended when the two Conestogas crossed the stream and rattled to a stop at the same spot in the cottonwoods where the women had camped before.

Several wolves feasting on the dead Kiowas fled at their approach. At the sight, Fargo went to each wagon and instructed the women driving to take the Conestogas several hundred yards west so the scavengers and the stench wouldn't pose a problem.

A grassy arm of land around which the stream curved afforded a fine stopping place. The wagons were parked on the north side, forming a barrier between their new camp and the trees. With the women busily tending to the stock and gathering wood for the fire, Fargo rode off on the Ovaro and made a wide circuit around their stopping place, insuring there were no Indians or other nasty surprises lurking in the vicinity.

Fargo was on his way back when a pair of deer darted from cover on his right. He had the Sharps across his thighs when they bolted, and in a flash the rifle was to his shoulder and his finger on the trigger. He tracked the largest of the pair with his sights. Then, at a range of sixty yards, he fired, whereupon the deer, a buck in its prime, crashed to the earth in a jumble of limbs.

The women had their own guns in hand when he returned. They had heard the shot and feared the worst. On seeing the buck, they broke out their knives and did a tolerable job of butchering the carcass, all except Danette, who wasn't allowed to do more than breathe. Her friends were mothering her to death, catering to her every whim, and she was lapping up the attention like a prissy cat lapped up milk.

Fargo feasted that night on well-done venison, hot coffee, and tasty biscuits. Sue had told her companions he knew their secret, so all were relaxed and carefree around him. Gone was the air of mystery, the atmosphere of tension. They joked with him and confided their hopes for their futures. They also revealed more about Tom Orland, about the many beatings they had suffered, and other mistreatment.

Stars dominated the heavens when, one by one, the weary women turned in. Susan Walker offered to take the first watch. She sat by Fargo for a while, telling him about the man she was going to marry, one Kyle Bechman, and how Bechman had saved up enough money for a down payment on their very own house.

Fargo knew more than he cared to know about her fiancé

when he excused himself and spread out his bedroll in the shadows to the south of the fire. Should unwanted visitors show up, he didn't want to be lying out in the open, a sitting duck for their guns or arrows. He sat down and reached for his right boot to tug it off, but stopped on hearing his name whispered from the inky strip of grass to his left. "Sue?" he responded.

"Yes. Come here a minute."

Rising, Fargo picked up the Sharps and moved through the gloom until he saw her standing beside the stream, her back to him. "What's the matter?" he whispered. "Did you hear something?"

"No."

"Then why did you call me?" Fargo asked, halting right behind her. "What's wrong?"

"Not a thing," Sue replied softly. She turned slowly, a languid smile on her full lips, and her hands reached up for his shoulders.

Fargo was flabbergasted to see the dark outline of her rifle on the grass beside her and to discover she had unbuttoned the top of her dress, uncovering her ripe breasts. "What is this?" he blurted.

"Can't you guess?" Sue said seductively, taking the Sharps from his unresisting fingers and placing it down next to her rifle. She pressed her lush body against his, her warm breath fanning his face, her mouth poised invitingly near his. "Now why don't you make up for that time in St. Louis, big man?" she proposed, and her mouth found his.

13

As with most men, there were times when women did things that completely astounded Skye Fargo. This was one of those times. He would have thought Sue would rather keep herself properly aloof until they arrived in Mountain City, yet here she was running her hands over his body and passionately kissing him. Never one to pass up an invitation, he responded in kind, but when she broke for air he commented, "Not ten minutes ago you were talking my ear off about your husband-to-be. Now this?"

Sue touched a finger to his chin, then traced it along his jaw to his neck. "Have you ever had one last drink before going off somewhere?"

"Who hasn't?"

"Think of this as my last drink," Sue said. Her lips closed on his again and locked there. Her tongue flicked over his gums and teeth.

Fargo got her meaning. She wanted him, wanted him badly. He would be her final fling before she tied the knot, and if that was how she wanted it, it was fine with him. He cupped her buttocks and pulled her hard against him. His mouth circled her left earlobe, his tongue swirled her neck. Gradually his mouth worked its way down from the ear, inside her dress, and to her left nipple, which hardened even as he touched it. Sucking hard, he prompted a low groan from deep in her throat. He brought his right hand up to cover her right breast and worked on both globes simultaneously.

"Oh, Lord!" Sue said breathlessly. "I'd almost forgotten how good this feels!"

Fargo decided to remind her—with a vengeance. He rubbed and tweaked her breasts for minutes, delighting in the way she quivered and rubbed against him, in her fevered panting in his ear. She was much livelier than Danette had been, always moving her body this way or that, doing those hundred and one little things that drove a man to the brink of madness. Sue was the type of woman who loved sex and made no complaints about her untamed desires. Would one man ever be able to satisfy her cravings? Probably, Fargo reflected, because she was also the type of person who stuck with something once she set her mind to it.

Sue had one hand at the back of his neck and was stroking it while her other hand dallied over the length and width of his thighs. She knew exactly where to touch to increase his hunger, all the sensitive spots that transformed the most mild-mannered of men into volcanic cauldrons of sheer lust.

Neither of them made much noise, other than sighs and whispers and gasps. They were too close to the wagons. One involuntary cry would bring the other women on the run.

Entwined, they kissed and petted and pressed, each fanning the inner flames of the other. Fargo lifted the hem of her dress to her waist, did likewise with her underclothes, and draped his hand on her inner thigh. Her skin trembled under his palm. When he elevated his hand to her crack, she threw back her head and exhaled loudly, her mouth working soundlessly.

Fargo found her hot, moist, and ready. He took her standing up, simply by unfastening his pants, freeing his pole, and feeding it into her slit inch by engorged inch. Sue's hands were everywhere, silently urging him on. Her mouth covered his face with scores of kisses.

"Fargo," she whispered when he was all the way in at last, "screw me silly."

"I aim to please."

Rising on his toes, Fargo began a pumping motion, his hands on top of her shoulders to hold her in place. Her inner walls sheathed his manhood as if the two had been made for one another. She nibbled on his mouth, on his throat, her fingers in his hair. Somewhere along the line she bumped off his hat.

Fargo didn't care. He continued thrusting upward and then settling slowly down to the ground, doing this over and over, sending erotic lightning shooting through their loins. His pole was like a rock and it seemed he could go on forever.

Suddenly Sue clasped him anew and shook from head to

toe. "I'm coming, Fargo. God, I'm coming!" she whispered fiercely.

That she was. Fargo felt her gush. Her release served as his own trigger, and with pinpoints of light bursting before his eyes, he pumped furiously into her. Locked mouth to mouth, they coasted to an eventual stop and stood shaking with the intensity of the aftermath.

"Thank you," Sue said in due course.

"Any time."

"Never again. You're the last, except for Kyle."

"Lucky Kyle," Fargo said, pecking her cheek. He eased his organ out of her and hiked his pants up. A pleasant lassitude made him want to curl into a ball right on the spot and sleep for a week or two.

Sue smoothed her dress and patted her hair into place. "If the others knew I did this they'd be terribly disappointed. I've been telling them for months that we have to control ourselves, that we have to prove ourselves worthy of the men we're going to marry." She glanced at the Conestogas. "That we have to be perfect ladies."

"You're not married yet," Fargo said as he stooped to retrieve the Sharps and his hat, "so don't be so hard on yourself. Once you are, I bet you'll make as good a wife as you did a whore."

"I hope you're right," Sue said earnestly, and kissed him. "That was sweet of you to say." She pursed her lips. "I can't get over it. You're not at all like I thought you'd be."

"So folks have been telling me lately," Fargo responded. "Seems I'll have to polish up my reputation." Turning, he scanned the wagons, and when he saw no one, he gave Sue a fleeting squeeze and returned to his bedroll. It had been an eventful, difficult day, and he was glad to finally be lying down to sleep. Closing his eyes, he folded his hands on his chest and wondered if the new day would be as rewarding as the past two had been. Catherine, after all, hadn't been able to satisfy her craving the other night when Sue interrupted them. Maybe she'd like to. He chuckled softly at the thought, reflecting again that his decision to guide these women had been one of the smartest things he'd ever done.

As if to indicate otherwise, from out of the cool night came the mournful howl of a prowling wolf.

* * *

The tops of the cottonwoods were rustling in the wind when Fargo awakened shortly before sunrise. None of the women were abroad yet other than Audris, who was on watch. She was adding branches to the fire.

Fargo slowly rose and adjusted his gunbelt. He'd slept with the Colt strapped around his waist and the Sharps at his side, a precaution that had saved his life more than once. The rifle in hand, he strolled over. "Morning. All quiet?"

Audris looked up with a start. "Goodness, you scared me! I didn't even hear you come up."

"Sorry."

"You're awful light on your feet for such a big man," Audris said, her gaze running admiringly down his body and stopping just below his belt.

"Force of habit," Fargo said. He tapped the coffee pot and almost burned his finger.

"I just made a new batch," Audris said. She hastily grabbed a cup and filled it for him, then held it out with an enticing smile. "If there's anything else I can do for you, anything at all, just let me know."

Fargo matched her frank stare and responded, "I'll keep that in mind." He sipped his coffee and grinned, certain the day was off to a fine start.

Within minutes Catherine and Rita had joined them. Shortly thereafter Sue and Danette stepped down, Danette full of vigor and vim, Sue with her hair disheveled and looking as if she hadn't gotten a minute's sleep.

Breakfast was kept short. Once the mules were hitched, the group headed out, bearing northward, Fargo in front. Clouds scuttled by overhead, promising relief from the heat. By midmorning it was drizzling, so the ladies donned their bonnets and wraps. Fargo simply pulled his hat lower.

The sky had not cleared by the time they made camp that night beside the main trail at the very spot where the two buffalo hunters had surprised them. Fargo collected wood from the stand of trees but had nothing else to do, as there was enough deer meat remaining for their supper. He sat and listened to the women talk about the dreams they had for their new lives, and before they retired he wished them all well.

Much to Fargo's disappointment, none of the five paid him a nocturnal visit or called him into the trees. He was able to sleep the whole night through. Then, thoroughly refreshed, his belly full, he took the point, resuming their westward trek. The women were in fine spirits, joking and laughing.

Clouds were once again the order of the day. More rain fell, a light sprinkle that pattered on the canvas tops and made the mules and horses glisten.

Fargo hadn't gone far when he noticed fresh hoof prints, made by five horses within the past twenty-four hours. The mounts had all been shod, which eliminated Indians. And they had been in a hurry, as demonstrated by the countless clods of dirt their driving hoofs had churned up. The tracks might have been made by anyone, but Fargo knew better. Orland and his men were up ahead.

Without being too obvious, Fargo shucked the Sharps and placed it across his legs. He also loosened the Colt in its holster and checked to be certain the Arkansas toothpick was snugly in place. None of the women noticed. Catherine and Rita were driving the Conestogas, Danette was inside the first one resting, and Sue and Audris were riding together behind the wagons, leading the spare horses.

Fargo constantly surveyed the horizon but saw no sign of riders. At the rate Orland had been traveling, his gang must be fifteen or twenty miles ahead, Fargo deduced. They posed little danger to the women unless they turned around.

At least Justis and Eb had done one thing right by disguising the point where the wagons had left the main trail. Orland and company had missed it, sure enough, and were likely assuming that some of the older ruts made by wagons that had passed by a week or two ago were the tracks left by the two Conestogas. Thank goodness, Fargo mused, that Orland's men were all city boys who knew next to nothing about tracking!

Toward noon Fargo called a brief halt to rest the mules. The drizzle had not yet let up, and the earth gave off a musty, dank scent that reminded Fargo of the lush forests of the Pacific Northwest. He was scratching the Ovaro's chin, his eyes fixed to the west, when Sue approached.

"It just occurred to me that we haven't paid you any of the money I promised."

"I trust you."

"If you want, I'll climb in the wagon and fetch the handbag," Sue offered. "We had to give it a washing after we found it on Eb, stuffed down his pants. I swear, that man had more lice and fleas than a mongrel dog."

"There's no need to give it to me right this minute," Fargo stressed. "It's a long way to the Rocky Mountains. You'll have plenty of time to pay up." He lowered his voice so none of the others would overhear his next remark. "Besides, if I was any kind of a gentleman, the other night would be payment enough."

Sue didn't grin at the joke. Instead, she frowned and replied, "That's been bothering me some. I wasn't very fair to you, was I?"

"In what way?"

"I used you. All I wanted was to satisfy my hunger. I never took your feelings into account."

"Do you hear me bellyaching?" Fargo laughed. "Hell, more women should use me like that. When my time comes, I'll die a happy man."

Joining in the laughter, Sue put a hand on his arm. "You're a prize, Trailsman. It's too bad I didn't get to know you that time back in St. Louis."

"It wouldn't have changed things," Fargo said. "You're the marrying kind. I'm not."

The reminder had a sobering effect. "I'll hand over the money later then," Sue said, and rejoined her friends.

Fargo gripped the saddle horn and swung astride the pinto. Why was it, he wondered, that some women thought they had a claim on a man once they went to bed with him? Give him women like Adeline any day, women who enjoyed frolicking under the blankets for the sheer fun of it and who didn't try to burn their brand on the man afterward.

Soon the Conestogas were rolling again. Fargo cautioned the women to stay on their guard, then he rode several miles in advance of the wagons, checking the trail. There was no indication that Orland, Bell, and the rest had slowed down. The hardcases were still well to the west, which should have reassured Fargo that all was well, but didn't.

That night camp was made in the open, not by choice, but because there was no vegetation other than grass to be seen anywhere. Fargo made sure the women built a small fire and pointed out that they should avoid making any loud noises as sounds carried great distances on the prairie.

Everyone turned in shortly after supper so they could get an early start the next day. Fargo lay on his blankets and stared at the heavens for hours, unable to sleep, bothered by an unshakable feeling of unease. He'd had such premonitions before and they'd always proven to be right, so he was extra vigilant in the morning when they proceeded on their trek.

The clouds were gone at last. Brilliant sunshine bathed the shimmering grass, and in the light of the new day Fargo's fears seemed unwarranted. He chided himself for having a bad case of nerves, yet no matter how hard he tried to relax, he met with no success.

Nightfall found them resting beside another isolated stand of trees, the wagons positioned at right angles to one another, forming a protective barrier in which the mules and horses were confined. Fargo ate little although he was famished. After the meal, he made several circuits of the camp and the trees. As he reentered the ring of firelight for the third time, Sue and Danette met him.

"We want to know what's bothering you," Sue informed him.

"Yeah," Danette chimed in. "You've got us all jumping at shadows. Do you know something we don't?"

Fargo hesitated. He'd refrained from saying anything about the tracks before this because he hadn't wanted to needlessly upset them but, now that he thought about it, he figured they had a right to know. "Orland and his bunch are a day in front of us."

The pair were visibly shocked.

"Why didn't you tell us sooner?" Sue demanded. "Were you going to wait until we ran into them and let us find out the hard way?"

"Typical man," Danette said, smirking. "They don't think we're able to take care of ourselves, so they're always looking out for us poor, helpless little females."

"I suppose I should have said something," Fargo conceded. "You can tell the rest. Then make sure two of you stand guard at all times. And never let anyone go off alone."

Sue scanned the encampment. "If Tom and his hired guns are a day ahead of us, why are you so worried?"

"I wish to hell I knew."

Fargo slept fitfully. The chirping of birds roused him as the sky to the east brightened slightly. Sitting up, he smoothed his ruffled hair, put on his hat, and stood. Catherine and Rita were by the fire, warming their hands, so he walked over. "See or hear anything unusual?" he asked.

"No," Catherine answered. "It was as quiet as could be."

The five women were subdued as they ate and harnessed the mules. Fargo once again took the lead, riding a dozen yards in front of the first lumbering Conestoga. As the sun slowly rose to his rear, the prairie in front of him glistened like the surface of the ocean. To the south a herd of antelope bounded off. To the west was nothing but the straight scar of the trail bordered by gently waving grass.

Fargo rose in the stirrups for a better view. As he did, one of the wagon wheels began to squeak loudly. He glanced at the offending wheel, debating whether to stop and apply axle grease. It sounded as if it needed greasing badly; if neglected, the hub might seize up. He settled into the saddle and lifted the reins to wheel the Ovaro, when all of a sudden his hat was plucked from his head by an invisible hand. A heartbeat later, the blast of a rifle shot rolled across the plain.

"Take cover!" Fargo yelled, hunching over the pinto and applying his spurs. He heard another shot and something snatched at his shoulder. Then he was sweeping around the first wagon and reining up. With a sharp tug, he freed the Sharps. Leaning to the side, he grabbed the back of the first Conestoga and pulled himself over the loading gate onto the bed. Danette was on her knees on a thick blanket, gaping at Rita who still sat on the seat, frozen with fear.

"Get down, damn it!" Fargo bellowed, and dashed past Danette. He was none too gentle about hauling Rita from her perch. Then, crouching behind the seat, he peered out over the top, seeking the rifleman.

"Orland and his men have found us!" Danette exclaimed.

"At least one of them has," Fargo replied. And that puzzled him. He was sure the same rifle had fired both shots, but if so, where were the rest of Orland's gunmen? What was just one doing out there?

"What do we do?" Danette asked.

"Sit tight," Fargo answered, scouring the prairie intently. He saw neither the rifleman nor the man's mount. Sinking down, he worked his way to the rear to check on the others.

Sue was crouched in the second Conestoga, her face framed by the canvas. Catherine and Audris, both on horseback, had sought safety behind her wagon, and their heads were visible at the back opening as they craned their necks to see past her. "Are you hurt?" she called out.

"No," Fargo responded.

A rifle appeared in Sue's hand. "All of us can shoot fairly well. I say we make a run for it."

"In these oversized turtles?" Fargo said, giving the gate a solid smack. "We wouldn't cover a hundred yards."

"None of Orland's bunch would shoot us. He wants us alive so he can take us back and show his other girls what happens to those who buck him."

"They don't want me alive," Fargo mentioned. He pointed at her team. "And whoever it is might shoot a few of the mules to stop us. Do you want to take the risk?"

Sue shook her head. "But we can't simply sit here."

No, they couldn't, Fargo mentally agreed, and leaned back to ponder their predicament. The nearest sanctuary of any kind was the stand of trees, now several hundred yards east of them. If the gunman could be kept busy, the women would have a chance to reach cover. He relayed the idea to Sue.

"And how do you figure to keep him preoccupied?" she wanted to know.

"Leave that to me," Fargo said. "You just be ready to turn your wagon around and go like blazes once I do." He faced Danette, who wore her anger like a mask, and Audris, who was trying valiantly to be brave but whose lips couldn't stop quivering. "Can the two of you handle this one?"

"If we can't," Danette said, "I'll throw it over my shoulders and carry the damn thing."

With a nod, Fargo slipped over the side. He crouched under the floorboards to scan the plain again but had no better luck than previously. The rifleman was well hidden. Straightening, he grasped the Ovaro's reins, then ran for the second wagon with the short hairs at the nape of his neck tingling every step of the way. Oddly, there was no shot. Either the rifleman hadn't spotted him or the man was busy changing position.

Once behind the second Conestoga, Fargo tied the pinto and walked to the spare horses. For what he had in mind he wasn't about to use the Ovaro and risk having it be hit by a bullet meant for him. He picked one of the Kiowa war horses, the one that had given Danette such a hard time.

Sue had moved to the back of her wagon. "You be careful, Trailsman. We've all taken a liking to you, and we'd hate to have you die on our account."

"You're not the only ones," Fargo said. "Don't worry. I'm not about to die when I haven't been paid yet." With a comforting smile, he was off, galloping southward, hoping to draw the rifleman's fire and give the women the opening they needed. He had gone only twenty yards when the ambusher opened up, the rifle cracking to the southwest. The whizz of the bullet prompted him to employ the same Sioux tactic he had employed against the Kiowas. He slid to one side and hung on for dear life.

To Fargo's rear there were shouts mixed with the cracks of whips. The women were doing as he'd directed, but they'd need another minute to swing the sluggish Conestogas completely around. Could he hold out that long?

Again the rifle blasted. Fargo spotted a telltale puff of smoke over a hundred and fifty yards away just as the war horse shook to the blow of the bullet. Seemingly unaffected, mane and tail flying, it sped onward with him clinging fast. A look to the right showed the two wagons were halfway around. Just a little bit farther ought to do it!

But the rifleman was persistent.

Fargo felt the war horse shake again. He was set to let go and shove to safety when the animal began to fall. A hoof struck him in the leg. The ground rushed up to meet him. He threw up an arm to shield his head, felt his other hand slipping off the Sharps, and then crashed down with such stunning force that he thought he was bursting apart.

Fargo didn't lose consciousness, but for all the pain he felt it might have been better if he had. Dimly, he knew that the hind end of the horse was lying on top of his legs. He also knew he'd lost the Sharps. The blinding sun started him blinking as he raised his head to look down at himself, so he screened his eyes with a palm.

The Kiowa mount was dead, a puddle of blood spreading out from under it. Several yards off lay the Sharps.

Fargo clenched his teeth and tried to pull his legs free but the weight was too great. He managed to sit up by leaning on an elbow. The surrounding grass was inches higher than his head, effectively concealing him from the rifleman for the moment. Twisting at the waist, he smiled on seeing both wagons close to the trees. The ruse had worked. Now all he had to do was reach the stand alive himself.

Gripping one of the horse's heavy forelegs, Fargo lifted and strained until he was red in the face. He moved the leg a few inches, yet failed to shift the hindquarters enough to extricate himself. The feat seemed impossible.

Thwarted, Fargo sank back and reflected. Since he couldn't lift the horse, there had to be another way. Curling forward, he slid his right hand underneath the dead animal to determine how far down he could reach. His fingers touched the top of his boot but could go no farther.

Girding his arm, Fargo thrust his fingers half an inch deeper. His shoulder ached terribly and his backbone shrieked in torment, but he refused to give up. Again he thrust, gaining another fraction. He rested his forehead on the horse's leg, tried to shut out the nearly overpowering smell of blood, and kept on alternately thrusting and relaxing, thrusting and relaxing, until his fingertips slipped under the edge of his boot and made contact with the Arkansas toothpick.

Ten minutes went by. Fifteen. By exercising patience and self-control, Fargo was able to wrap two fingers around the hilt. Then, his shoulder joint throbbing, he wrenched the knife from its sheath. Still he had to struggle, gradually working his hand back out. After an eternity he tugged it free and sank down in relief.

That was when the nearby grass rustled.

Fargo stiffened and raised his head. Thirty feet away, a vague shape was moving toward him. He dropped the knife, palmed his Colt, and took hasty aim. At the same instant, the shape blended into the grass and vanished. It had to be the rifleman, coming to finish him off. Once the man saw that he was helplessly pinned, he'd be dead in no time. Unless . . .

Lying down again, Fargo adjusted his right arm so that the Colt was partially hidden by his back. He went completely limp, feigning death, and breathed as shallowly as he could so his chest wouldn't rise and fall with each breath. Ears pricked for the slightest sounds, he waited. But not for long.

The rustling grew louder and louder, then abruptly stopped. Perhaps a minute elapsed where there was no sound other than the faint whispering of the breeze. Then came the stealthy pad of a single footstep.

Fargo held his breath, knowing the killer was creeping toward him. He had to let the man get so close he couldn't miss, but it was nerve-racking to lie there and do nothing when the rifleman might put another slug into him at any second to be certain he was dead. The footsteps were much nearer. His lungs beginning to ache, Fargo cracked his eyelids a fraction.

It was Bell. The tall gunman had his rifle at waist height, leveled unerringly on the Trailsman's midsection. He glanced at the pool of blood, then at the war pony, and back at Fargo. Slowly he straightened. The rifle barrel drooped. "I reckon you had to learn the hard way," he said to himself. "Too bad we couldn't have done this man to man. I would have taken you."

Fargo could hold his breath no longer. He snapped up, inhaling as he did, his gun hand a blur. "Here's your chance," he declared.

Bell reacted swiftly, his rifle rising as he dropped into a crouch, his finger curling around the trigger. He was still applying pressure when the first slug tore through his chest, spinning him half around. A second slug caught him below his left arm, staggering him. His face misshapen in rage, he tried desperately to swing around, to bring his rifle to bear, but a third slug, striking him above his ear, ended his days as a killer for hire. Mouth agape, he toppled.

Skye Fargo exhaled, his arm sinking to his side. "A man should never work his mouth when he should be working his trigger," he commented softly. Then he quickly replaced the spent cartridges and shoved the Colt back into his holster.

Gripping the toothpick, Fargo bent forward and jabbed the slender blade into the packed earth under his right leg. Ordinarily he wouldn't think of using the knife to dig with, but there was nothing else he could use. And he had to free himself before Orland and the rest of his men showed up, as they were bound to do.

Slowly the blazing sun climbed on high as Fargo dug and dug, brushing the excess dirt aside with his forearm. His shoulder muscles were throbbing when, after loosening a large clod, he discovered he could move his right leg a few inches. Energized by this small accomplishment, he poked and stabbed in a frenzy, and shortly thereafter, had removed enough dirt to pull his right leg all the way out. Once that was done, the left leg was easy to free.

Fargo would have loved to lie down and rest, but he dared not. While he had been digging, he'd been thinking about why Bell had been all alone, and a possible explanation had occurred to him. Orland must have realized the wagons had turned off the trail at some point and was trying to find exactly where. His men had fanned out to cover more ground as they searched, and Bell had ridden the farthest east.

Reclaiming the Sharps and scooping up Bell's rifle, Fargo hurried toward the stand of trees. He had no doubt the gunshots had been heard by some or all of Orland's men and that the rest would show up at any second. He wanted to be ready for them when they did.

Unfortunately, Fargo's legs refused to move very fast. Being pinned had cut off the circulation, and now both were tingling fiercely. He had to concentrate to keep them moving and disregarded pangs that shot from his ankles to his hips. The three hundred yards he had to cover were more like miles, but presently he was close enough to see the women waiting for him at the prairie's edge.

Sue and Danette smiled and waved.

Fargo waved back. By now the tingling had lessened and he could run without too much difficulty. Forty yards were all that remained when the women started shouting and hopping up and down and pointing at something behind him. Fully aware of what he would see, Fargo glanced over his right shoulder.

Tom Orland and four gunhands were five hundred yards out, on the trail, and closing swiftly in a tightknit group. They had the look of men who meant business. Several held rifles, the barrels glinting in the sunlight, and the others were pulling theirs out.

"Hurry!" Sue beckoned.

Danette, never one for keeping quiet, added, "Move your fanny, Trailsman, unless you care to lose it!"

Fargo did just that, pushing his legs to their limits. He was winded and ready to collapse when he reached the trees and leaned his back against a trunk. Orland's men were now about four hundred yards off and still clustered together. "Fools," he muttered.

"What's that?" Catherine asked.

Instead of answering, Fargo gave her Bell's rifle, then he wedged the Sharps to his shoulder and moved a stride from the tree. His legs were weak, his lungs aching, but he was able to hold the Sharps steady enough to take careful aim.

"Why waste the bullet?" Danette inquired. "They're too far out for you to do more than give them a scare."

"Think so?" Fargo said, tossing his head to shake a bead of sweat out of his left eye. He licked his dry lips and pressed his cheek to the rifle. Only then did he realize Tom Orland was riding behind the other gunmen rather than in front of them, and try as he might he couldn't get a clear bead on the pimp. So he settled for the lead rider, cocked the Sharps, set the trigger and, when he had held the barrel firm for a three count, he fired.

The gunman threw out his hands and catapulted over the rump of his animal. Instantly Orland and the other two scattered, breaking to the right and left. They also opened fire, and although they weren't the marksmen Fargo was,

145

some of their shots zipped into the trees close to the women.

"Hide out!" Fargo bellowed, giving Sue and Danette shoves that propelled them into the stand. Back-pedaling, he crouched low and watched the three killers continue to fan out around the trees. Their intent wasn't hard to guess. They'd take up positions at three points of the compass and flatten in the grass, effectively preventing escape. Fargo and the women would be trapped.

Breaking into a run, Fargo made for the south border of the stand. He hoped to get another shot off before the trio went to ground. Just one shot would be all that was needed if he could slay Tom Orland. With their boss dead, the other two were bound to head for parts unknown. But he was too slow. He came up behind the last few trees and saw Orland already swinging down. With a swat Orland sent his mount running southward, then disappeared in the grass.

"Damn," Fargo said in irritation. The third gunman, a beefy killer in a brown hat, was still in the saddle, racing eastward. Fargo quickly plucked a new cartridge out, fed it into the Sharps, and hastily tried to fix his sights on the man. Just as he did, the rider reined up, leaped down, and sank from view.

"The third one is north of us, Skye."

Fargo turned to find Susan and Danette had trailed him. "He's there to keep an eye on the wagons and stop us in case we should try to leave."

"We're in a fine fix," Susan said.

"I don't see why you're worried," Danette disagreed. "They're not about to shoot us. You said so yourself. And we have plenty of food and water, while they don't, so there's no way they can try to starve us out or make us give up because of thirst." She chuckled. "I'd say we're sitting pretty, and Mr. Tom Orland has overplayed his hand."

"Maybe," Susan said, her tone lacking conviction.

Fargo wasn't so sure, either. Orland knew the women had water and food, so he wouldn't be content to try and wait them out. The only way for Orland to win was to force the women from hiding. How he would do it was the big question. "Get everyone together," he directed. "I'll show each of you where to take up your positions. We have to be ready when they make their move."

Nodding, Susan spun and was about to walk off when a harsh hail from out on the prairie rooted her in place.

"Sue! I know you can hear me!" Orland yelled. "Give up, right this minute, and I'll go easy on you gals. If you don't, you'll regret it."

Susan opened her mouth to answer, but Danette beat her to the punch.

"Go to hell, Tom! You're wasting your breath! We're not about to let you get your dirty hands on us, now or ever!"

There were several seconds of silence, then Orland replied. "Danette, was that you? You always did think with your mouth, you dumb whore." He paused. "Since Sue thinks she's too good to answer me, make sure she understands that if she doesn't do as I say, none of you will leave there alive."

Danette was all set to respond when Susan held up a hand, silencing her, and shouted, "This is Sue, Tom. Spell out what you mean."

"Just this, dear heart. I've tried to be reasonable with you. I've tried to make you see the mistake you're making, but words and slapping you around haven't worked. You just don't care that my reputation will suffer if I let you get away with this, and none of you give a damn about fulfilling your ends of our contracts. If you don't care, why the hell should I?"

"What are you saying?" Susan said.

"It should be obvious. My patience is at an end, woman. When I first came after all you gals, I figured to take you back, to make a lesson out of you for the others. But now I've changed my mind. You've given me too much trouble, you and that Trailsman of yours. So here's the way it is." Orland stopped, perhaps deliberately to draw out the suspense. "Unless you throw out your guns and come out in the open where we can see you, my boys and I are going to open fire and keep on shooting until every last one of you is dead."

"You wouldn't!"

"I don't need you alive to convince my other girls to toe the line," Orland answered. "All I have to do is take back your ring finger with that ruby ring you love so much. They'll get the point."

Susan glanced down at her left hand and touched the ring he had mentioned.

"You've brought this on yourselves," Orland shouted. "I'll give you five minutes to talk it over, then we cut loose. Don't think we won't. You should know me well enough, Sue, to know I'm a man who does what he says he'll do."

"The bastard!" Danette hissed.

Fargo motioned for them to move. "Get everyone into the middle of the stand. Hurry!" He turned back to the plain, seeking some sign of Orland. During all the yelling back and forth he had noticed that the wily pimp never stayed in one spot for very long, making it impossible to pinpoint his exact position. He waited in vain for a full minute, then whirled and sped to where the women were arguing heatedly.

"I say we do as Tom wants," Rita was saying. "We've done the best we could and it wasn't good enough. He won't do more than knock us around a little."

"I agree," Audris said. "This hasn't worked out as we thought it would. All the money we've spent, all the time and hard work we've put into making our dream come true, and what has it gotten us?"

Susan drew herself up to her full height and gave the two of them scathing looks. "It's gotten us over halfway to Mountain City, hasn't it? And for the first time in years we can all say we're free women, able to live our lives the way we want. You'd give that up? You'd give up the chance to marry and settle down?"

"I just don't want to die," Rita said.

Fargo strode forward to the center of their group and declared, "None of you will die if I can help it. Look around you." He gestured at the trees. "Orland and his men can fire all day and all night and not hit a thing if you stay down. He's playing a bluff, hoping to scare you into giving in. Are you going to let him?"

The five of them studied the stand for a bit, until Rita said, "You're right. And I'll bet he doesn't have much ammunition to spare, either. I'll stay if the rest of you do."

"Not me," Audris unexpectedly stated. Then, her dress swirling around her, she was off, bounding like a frightened doe toward the south side of the stand.

"No!" Sue cried.

"Stop her!" Danette yelled.

Fargo tried, but he only took two swift strides when Catherine accidentally stepped into his path and they collided.

Disentangling himself took no more than a few seconds, yet it was long enough to permit Audris to gain a wide lead. Sue and Rita were also in pursuit, although it was apparent neither were as fast as Audris and stood no hope of catching her. Danette, meanwhile, had sprinted a few feet, then halted and clutched her side.

The only one who stood a prayer of saving the young woman was Fargo. Once free of Catherine, he poured on the speed, rapidly overtaking Sue and Rita and passing them both. Ahead he glimpsed Audris's flying figure. She was wending among the trees with surprising agility, not hampered by her flowing dress at all. He began to doubt he could catch her before she reached the prairie, but he never slackened his pace. Soon he saw the high grass ahead of her. He saw her raise an arm and heard her shout.

"Tom! Tom! It's Audris! I'm coming out!"

And, the next moment, Fargo heard the crash of rifles and saw Audris buckle as hot lead smacked into her chest and face. He threw himself at the base of a tree as more bullets whined through the air and, shifting, he gestured for Sue and Rita to do the same. Sue promptly obeyed. Rita, horrified by the sight of Audris's bloody body sprawling to the earth, halted and froze, her mouth agape. Fargo clearly heard a slug thud into her shoulder and spin her around where she stood. Cursing, he launched himself through the air and tackled her, bearing her to safety in the shelter of a bush. More bullets struck nearby trees. Bits of bark and branches rained down. Then the firing ceased as abruptly as it had begun.

Rita was whimpering pathetically and tears were pouring down her cheeks. A trickle of blood flowed from her wound.

"Hang on," Fargo said, sliding his arms under her. Digging in his heels, he stood and headed for the center of their sanctuary. Susan joined him.

"How bad is she?"

"I don't know yet."

"What about Audris?" Sue asked, looking back, her face a chalky white.

"We'll bury her when there's time."

"She might still be alive."

"You know better. One of those shots hit her between the eyes."

Catherine and Danette saw them coming and hurried to meet them, spouting questions which Sue answered. They clammed up on learning that Audris was dead.

Fargo was too preoccupied to notice, working out what he should do next. Was it smarter to stay in the trees until Orland and his men ran low on ammo, he asked himself, or should he take the fight to them? One glance at Rita's anguished face made up his mind for him.

They were close to the center when a strident yell from Orland signaled another volley. Fargo dropped down. So did the women, and this time, since they were deeper into the trees, no one was hit. Some of the bullets came uncomfortably close, though, and once Catherine yelped when a wood chip flew from a tree, stinging her cheek.

At length the firing tapered off. Fargo hoisted Rita and ran the final few yards, depositing her in a narrow hollow between two trees where she would be safe from the gunfire. The others gathered around him.

Just then, from the prairie, rose the voice of Tom Orland. "Had enough yet, ladies? Or do we keep on chipping away until each and every one of you ends up like Audris? I'll give you two minutes to come to your senses."

"He shot her on purpose!" Sue exclaimed. "I thought it was an accident!" Her eyes sparkled with fury. "He made a mistake doing that. None of us will ever give up now."

"I'd like to slit the son of a bitch's throat," Danette said, shaking her fists in her rage.

"Leave the job to me," Fargo said grimly. Hefting the Sharps, he took several paces northward. "Do what you can for Rita, and remember to stay down."

"Where are you going?" Sue asked.

"To give my elbows and knees some exercise." Fargo crept through the stand until he spied the parked wagons. So far none of the horses or mules had been touched, but it wouldn't be long before Orland got the bright idea to use them to force the women into the open by shooting one every minute or so until the women surrendered.

Lowering onto his stomach, Fargo crawled forward until he was at the very last tree. Somewhere directly north of him lurked the third killer. If the man was down low in the grass, then it would be safe for Fargo to crawl across the open space between the stand and the Conestogas without fear of being discovered. If not, if the man was close to the wagons and could see the open stretch clearly, then the last sound Fargo would hear would be the blast of the gunman's rifle.

It was a risk Fargo had to take. The Sharps in front of him, Fargo slid from concealment, making for the nearest Conestoga. He barely breathed, the better to hear faint sounds from up ahead. The skin on his back tingled. His palms grew sweaty. Some of the animals looked at him, and he dreaded having one of them nicker and alert the gunman. One of the mules did stomp its hoof several times, but it made no other noise.

At the same instant, Tom Orland bellowed again. "Well, what's it going to be, Sue? Throw out your guns and come on out and there will be no hard feelings. I give you my word. As for the Trailsman, you leave him to us."

There was no answer from the women. Seconds dragged by, then Fargo was in the shadow of the wagon and rolling underneath it. He came to rest behind the rear wheel. Peering between the spokes, he sought the killer.

"You're making this awful hard on yourself," Orland shouted. "If that's the way you want it, fine."

Suddenly the air rocked once more to the booming of rifles. Fargo tensed, expecting the gunman on his side of the stand to join in, but to his disappointment the rippling plain was as serene as ever. Too bad, he reflected. He would have to do it the hard way, as usual.

Drawing his right knee up to his chest, Fargo reached down and slid the toothpick out. The firing to the south was dying down. Someone—Danette, he thought—was screaming curses at Orland, insulting the pimp, his mother, and all their ancestors back to the dawn of time.

Fargo had to get moving. Holding the slender knife in one hand and the heavy Sharps in the other, he crawled out from under the cover of the Conestoga and into the grass. Here he paused, and again every few feet thereafter, to look and listen.

The sun scorched Fargo's back. Dust got into his nose, threatening to make him sneeze. Small stones gouged his body every so often. All of this was of no importance. He devoted his entire attention to finding the gunman before the gunman spotted him. Twenty yards from the wagons, as he quietly parted the grass in front of him, a muffled cough gave his enemy away. He figured the killer lay less than fifteen feet off, to the northwest, so he swung to the northeast, working in a wide circle that eventually brought him up behind the unsuspecting hardcase.

Fargo had learned the craft of moving stealthily from the Sioux and others who were equally expert. When he wanted to, he could be as silent as his own shadow. This was one of those occasions. He was able to get within two yards of his quarry without being discovered. Then the unforeseen happened. The one element over which he had no control ruined his perfect stalk.

The gunman turned. Warned by that indefinable sixth sense men who lived by the gun often developed, he had felt rather than heard something behind him. And on seeing the Trailsman, he scrambled around, trying to bring his rifle into play.

Fargo let go of the Sharps and sprang. He wanted to take care of the killer quietly so Orland and the other man to the south wouldn't realize he was no longer in the trees, but in this he was foiled when the rifle the gunman held went off as he slammed into the man. They both crashed down, Fargo on top and driving his knife at the killer's chest. The rifle barrel deflected the blow. Twisting, Fargo stabbed at the man's neck but missed and the rifle stock rammed into his temple.

His head spinning, Fargo pushed to one side. He saw the gunman claw at a revolver. The man's movements seemed to be in slow motion, but Fargo's weren't as his right arm snapped back, then forward, and the Arkansas toothpick leaped from his fingers. The blade bit into the killer's throat, to the hilt. Screeching, the man grabbed the knife and pulled, which was the wrong thing to do. It was like popping the plug on a full keg of wine, only in this instance blood sprayed out instead of the fruit of the vine.

Fargo's hand fell on his Colt but he didn't clear leather. The gunman had forgotten all about him and was futilely trying to plug the hole in his neck with his fingers. Sputtering and convulsing, Orland's man died a slow, terrifying death. At the last his eyes gazed at Fargo as if begging for help, then the spark of life blinked out of them and the man slumped limp and motionless.

Speed was now essential. Fargo was certain Orland or the man in the brown hat would come to investigate the shot, and he had to be elsewhere when they did. Recovering the toothpick and the Sharps, he rose and hastened to the Conestogas, boosting himself into the one to which the Ovaro was tied. He crouched down and cocked the Sharps.

There were yells in the trees. The women were calling his name, wanting to know if he was all right.

Fargo wasn't about to answer when Orland or the last gunman or both might be close enough to hear. The women shouldn't be yelling anyway, since it confirmed for Orland that he had indeed left the stand. Annoyed by their carelessness, he could only hope it wouldn't prove his undoing.

The seconds grew into minutes. Fargo, becoming impatient, warily poked his head up to peek over the back of the wagon and almost instantly saw the man in the brown hat thirty feet away, creeping northward. As fate would have it, the man happened to be looking at the wagon and spied him at the same moment. Fargo jerked the Sharps up to fire but the gunman dived into the grass. Since to stay in the Conestoga now invited death, Fargo gripped the top of the gate and jumped. As he fell a rifle thundered and a slug tore into the wood beside him. He landed lightly on his feet, then hurtled to the left, into the grass which closed around him like a blanket.

Fargo worked his way eastward at a snail's pace, the cocked Sharps extended, his finger on the trigger. The gunman, by his reckoning, was either moving slowly toward him or else hurrying back to tell Orland that the third and last member of their gang must be dead. Suddenly the tops of a dozen slender blades about ten feet off swayed more than they should. At their base a dark object materialized.

Tucking his face to the stock, Fargo fixed his sights on the center of the form and fired. The grass erupted in a frenzy of violent shaking and rustling that lasted for the longest while. Then all was still once more. Palming the Colt, Fargo rose in a crouch and dashed forward, ready to finish the man off.

Another shot wasn't needed. The Sharps had blown a fist-sized hole in the man's chest, puncturing both lungs. Never again would the man in the brown hat hire his gun out to men like Tom Orland.

Fargo headed for the stand, reloading the Sharps as he ran. He was halfway there when Susan Walker appeared at the tree line, a rifle in hand. He glanced to the west to make sure Orland wasn't sneaking up on them from that direction. Then, reaching her side, he commented, "You should have stayed with the others."

"I thought you might need some help."

Tom Orland chose that moment to bellow at the top of his lungs, from somewhere south of the stand, "Webber? Rolman? Did you get him?" When neither of his killers responded, he roared, "Answer me, damn you! What happened?"

Dashing into the trees, Fargo slanted in the direction the voice came from. Now it was Orland against him, and he had an idea how he could end the affair once and for all, an idea that he put into practice when he came to a wide tree near the prairie. Tucking the Sharps under his left arm, he seized an overhead limb and pulled himself off the ground. Careful to keep the trunk between his body and the area where Orland was in hiding, he climbed high enough to command a bird's-eye view of the surrounding plain. Then, ever so cautiously, he peered around the trunk, confident he would spot Orland right away. And he did, but not where he expected.

Orland was over a hundred yards distant, on all fours, barreling through the grass in a beeline for his horse, which was grazing three hundreds yards from the stand.

Fargo elevated the rifle, then hesitated. It went against his grain to shoot anyone in the back. And the only part of Orland's body he could see clearly was his backside. Then Fargo thought of Sue and all the other women Orland had beaten. He thought of the ones like Martha Danbridge, who had been crippled for life, and Fargo took aim. Just as he did, Tom Orland suddenly, mysteriously, vanished.

It took a few seconds for Fargo to guess the reason. The pimp had stumbled on a gully, which might well bring him out close to his mount. Cursing, Fargo flew down the tree and hit the ground on the run. Sue was nearby. She looked at him quizzically as he shot past so he explained over his shoulder, "The bastard is getting away!"

The Ovaro's head was up when Fargo burst from the vegetation. He ran to the second wagon and leaped into the saddle, then, wrenching the reins loose, he wheeled the stallion and applied his spurs. Around the trees they swept, and there, four hundred yards off and riding hell-for-leather to the southeast, was Tom Orland.

"No you don't!" Fargo snarled, urging the pinto to go

faster. He had every confidence in the stallion's ability, but he could see that Orland's horse was no swayback. It was a fine sorrel with lean, muscular lines, and every indication of possessing great endurance. Catching it wouldn't be easy.

Tom Orland rode surprisingly well. Perhaps prodded by fear, he was handling his horse as well as a Texas cowboy. He repeatedly glanced back at the Trailsman and fingered the Starr double-action .44 on his left hip.

Fargo shoved his Sharps into the boot to free both of his hands for riding. Since he lacked a hat, his hair whipped in the wind and he had to squint in the harsh glare of the bright sunlight. He wisely kept his eyes fixed on Orland's gun hand as he tried hard to cut the distance between them, and it was well he did.

Orland had gone over half a mile when he came to a low knoll. Suddenly drawing rein at the top, he turned the sorrel broadside, drew his Starr, and snapped off two shots spaced so close together they sounded like one.

Skye Fargo wasn't caught napping. When he saw Orland turn, he bent forward so his torso was flush with the Ovaro's neck. Both shots went high, and Orland, his features livid, lashed the sorrel down the opposite side of the knoll. Fargo reached the same spot thirty seconds later. Like Orland, he reined up. But instead of drawing his Colt, he shucked the Sharps. Removing his left foot from the stirrup, he looped his leg over the saddle horn for added balance, then just sat there, watching the pimp flee.

Precious seconds elapsed. Fargo calmly studied the rear sight and adjusted it slightly to compensate for the range at which he was going to fire. He licked his right forefinger and raised it high to test the wind. Satisfied, he touched the stock to his right shoulder.

Far out on the prairie, Tom Orland looked and remembered the gunman shot from horseback earlier as his men approached the stand. He realized what the Trailsman was going to do, and in imitation of Fargo he lowered the upper half of his body over the sorrel's flying mane, positive no one could hit so small a target at such a distance.

Fargo checked the sun, then brushed a piece of grass from the rifle barrel. His gaze ran from the rear sight to the front sight and he leveled the gun to line them up properly. Then, at long last, he aimed at Orland, at a spot only a foot or so above the sorrel's rump. He took a deep breath, held it, steeled his arms, and lightly touched the trigger.

A quarter of a mile out, Tom Orland snapped bolt upright, his arms flung outward. A bloodcurdling scream tore from his lips, a scream that only ended when his head crunched onto the ground under the driving hoofs of the panicked sorrel.

And back on the knoll, the Trailsman slowly lowered the Sharps, gave the rifle an affectionate pat, and blew smoke from the tip of the barrel. "I reckon he got his in the end," he said to himself. Then, throwing his head back, he laughed long and hard.

Three days later, Fargo was well in advance of the Conestogas, trotting along the well worn trail, when he spotted five riders bearing down on him from the west. He immediately draped his right hand on his thigh, close to the Colt, and stopped.

The five saw him moments later and one of them gave a shout. They all slowed. Every man in the group sported a full beard. They wore either store-bought flannel shirts and overalls or homespun clothes, all in need of stitching, as was usually the case with the clothing of bachelors. A rifle rested in a scabbard on each saddle, but none of them made a move to unlimber a gun as they came to a weary stop in front of him.

"Howdy, mister," said a skinny man who wore a soft felt cap, a style popular with miners.

"Howdy yourself," Fargo responded.

"We don't mean to be bothering you, but we'd like to ask an important question."

"I'm listening."

"My name is Kyle Bechman," the skinny man disclosed. "This here is Angus McFee," he said, pointing at a burly redhead. "Him and me and all these boys are miners from Mountain City."

"You've come a long way," Fargo commented.

"That we have, but for a good reason. We're trying to find our sweethearts, who wrote us that they might be taking the trail between Abilene and Denver."

"That's right," Angus threw in. "And we were wonderin' if you might have come across them?"

"Come to think of it," Fargo said, suppressing a grin, "I

did see two wagons a while back with a lot of women on board."

"How far back?" Kyle asked excitedly.

"Not more than two miles—," Fargo answered, and never got to finish his statement because the miners were galloping like madmen to the east. Twisting, he watched them for a while, trying to decide whether he should turn around and go back. He thought of Susan Walker, Danette, and Catherine, and wondered if any of them talked in their sleep. Then, lifting the reins, he continued along the trail toward the setting sun and was soon lost in the haze.

LOOKING FORWARD!
The following is the opening
section from the next novel in the exiting
Trailsman series from Signet:

THE TRAILSMAN #145
CHEYENNE CROSSFIRE

*Wyoming Territory, 1860 . . . where justice is swift,
and a man's life can depend on a thread of memory
or snap at the end of a hangman's noose.*

The pain pounded in heavy waves through his head. Skye
Fargo lifted one hand to his forehead and rubbed it, coming
slowly awake. He pulled the bedclothes up higher and
turned onto his side. What had given him this headache?
He stretched his limbs beneath the sheets and nuzzled the
feather pillow. Maybe a little more sleep and the pain would
go away, he thought dully. He inhaled and came fully alert
at the unmistakable odor. Blood. Fresh. Nearby.

Fargo sat bolt upright, his head whirling and pounding.
Where the hell was he? He looked around.

He lay in a brass bed, in a large white room well-fur-
nished with carved dark wood. Late-morning light poured
through the fluttering lace curtains.

Sprawled across the floor lay a woman in a white gown,
face down, her long dark hair tangled. A dark rivulet of
blood snaked across the wide planks of the floor. There was
no question she was dead. And had been for a few hours.

Fargo rubbed his head again and smelled more blood. He
slowly put his hand down and saw that blood was on his
hands, smeared all over the sheets of the bed.

Fargo gazed about the room again, confused. He didn't

recognize it. Nothing, absolutely nothing was familiar to him. And his head hurt so much that thinking was painful. And who the hell was the dead woman?

Was it possible . . . ? His head reeled with the thought and he quickly put it away, flinging aside the bedclothes and rising.

He was stark naked. Fargo quickly crossed to the washstand and washed the blood off his hands and arms. His clothes hung over the back of a nearby chair. He dressed hastily, fighting the waves of black pain that continued to roll from one ear to the other inside his brain. All the while, he looked down at the woman's body. He found his ankle holster on the chair, but the knife that went in it was nowhere to be seen. The Colt was in its holster, which he buckled around him.

This had to be a bad dream, Fargo told himself, but he knew it wasn't.

He knelt down beside the woman's body and gently turned her over. She was pretty, dark brows against pale skin, a few freckles scattered across the bridge of her nose. Her cornflower-blue eyes, still open, were blank. Fargo closed them. Blood was smeared across her cheek.

Her white lace nightgown had been slit down the front. She had been garrotted, stabbed in the chest numerous times and then sliced open through the belly, her guts spilling out on the floor. Whoever had killed the woman had to have been a monster. Or have gone completely mad.

Fargo sat back on his heels, his mind racing, trying to remember anything about the girl, about the room. But he drew a blank. The memory was gone. Was it possible . . . ? He posed the question to himself again. Temporary insanity, madness? Was he capable of doing this? But even as he tried to imagine himself murdering the girl, he knew he didn't. And yet . . .

Fargo pulled a blanket from the bed and wound it around the girl's body. He bent down and lifted her in his arms. As he picked her up, he heard a clatter. His knife lay on the floor. Fargo carried her to the bed, laid her out, and covered her with a sheet.

The sound of a woman's voice from somewhere below him echoed down the hallway. He crossed to the door and opened it slowly, just a crack, peering out. A short hall, a couple of chairs, and a table with a globe lamp was all there was to see. He closed the door silently. There was no lock, so he pushed a chair under the knob. If someone, anyone, happened to come in, it would look for certain that he had murdered the girl. He needed time to figure out what had happened.

Fargo turned and surveyed the room. If he hadn't murdered the girl, then who had? And why was he being set up? And who was the girl anyway?

Fargo looked her over again and then noticed a small opal ring on one of her fingers. With a silent apology to the dead girl, he took it off her finger and examined it. Inside was inscribed "HMK, Always, LJK." He pocketed the ring. If he ever found the girl's relatives, he'd return it. Meanwhile, it might be a clue to who she was and what had happened here.

Fargo searched the bureau and found only a silver brush and mirror, lingerie, and various lotions. Her dresses and coats hung in the closet. He looked for a purse or a handbag, but there was none to be found.

On the writing desk were a pen and inkwell along with a small supply of plain stationery and envelopes. He picked up the top sheet and held it flat so that the light would fall across it. Sometimes the pen nib made an impression on the second sheet that could be read. No such luck. Fargo replaced the sheet of paper. He picked up the curved blotter and turned it over, hoping to find blotter paper with ink stains in the shape of a name, or anything. But the blotter paper had been removed. Whoever had set him up had done a damn thorough job, Fargo thought to himself. With the exception of the ring, not a clue of the girl's identity remained.

Fargo crossed to the window and looked out. The sloping tin roof glittered in the sun. Below he saw a quiet stable yard. Standing tethered to a fence just beneath the window was his Ovaro. And it was saddled. Fargo strained his memory again for any shred of memory of the stable yard. Nothing.

He swore. It was all being set up just right, he thought grimly, his head still in agony. Here he was in the room with the girl. His knife had been used to murder her. His horse stood waiting for him to make a getaway. That was what they expected. That's what they wanted. Well, he thought, that's not what they would get.

And who the hell were *they* anyway?

There wasn't time for another thought. A woman's light footsteps tapped hurriedly down the hall, pausing on the other side of the door. The doorknob jiggled as she tried to open it. The chair held. The doorknob jiggled again, impatiently.

Whoever it was stepped back from the door and waited a long moment. Then she screamed.

Instantly, Fargo heard the pounding of heavy feet running up the stairs.

"What's the matter?" a gruff voice called out. He heard other men's voices. There were at least four of them. And the woman.

Fargo looked about. There was no escape, except by rolling down the roof and riding off on the Ovaro. But that's what they wanted him to do.

"The door!" the woman responded. "I can't get it open!"

There was an awkward silence.

"Hannah?" the woman called. "Hannah? Are you all right?"

"Stand back," one of the men shouted. A gunshot exploded the doorknob and latch, knocking the chair sideways. The door suddenly flew open and a huge man filled the doorframe, his gun drawn. His face was burned carmine and chiseled deep by lines, like a streambed's rivulets. His eyes were coal-black, his ebony hair snowy at the temples. A marshal's badge was on his leather vest.

"What the hell is going on in here?" the marshal shouted. Fargo noted that he glanced first at the floor where the girl had lain and where her blood still darkened the wood. Then his eyes swept the room and saw the form under the sheet on the bed. Finally, he locked eyes with Fargo, who stood by the window.

"You murderer!" the marshal said.

Fargo's eyes narrowed.

"Why do you say that?" Fargo asked, his voice cool.

The huge man was taken aback and gaped for a moment.

He took a step toward the bed and pulled back the sheet and blanket, revealing the girl. The plump blonde woman with a pug nose who had been standing right behind the marshal came inside the room after him. She spotted the murdered girl and shrieked. Three other men crowded in behind her and stood gawking.

"Murder!" she screamed. "Arrest him! Hang him!"

Fargo didn't move. He knew his life hung on how he reacted. Guilty men fled. Innocent men didn't. And he was innocent. With every passing moment he was more sure of it.

"I didn't kill her," Fargo said. "And I can prove it." The marshal stared back at him, his mouth open.

Fargo faced him down, his lake-blue eyes cold, his chiseled jaw set and unyielding. He was bluffing. He couldn't prove it. But a bluff might buy him time. And time would bring him information. And that might save his life.

"What . . . what do you mean you can prove it?" the marshal said. "You came into town last night. You got drunker and drunker. Then you came up here with Hannah. Of course you knifed her."

"How do you know it was a knife?" Fargo asked.

"I got eyes don't I?" the marshal sneered. "She's cut up, ain't she?"

"Could have been a hatchet. Or a razor," Fargo said.

The marshal barked a laugh.

"He's crazy," the woman whispered so that everyone in the room could hear her. "Just shoot him."

The marshal exchanged looks with the woman and tightened the grip on his pistol.

As the shot exploded, Fargo dove sideways. The bullet grazed his shoulder as he drew the Colt and fired in one swift motion, aiming at the marshal's leg. His pistol clicked. Empty. Fargo shouted, enraged at his own stupidity as he hit the floor and rolled once. Of course, they'd taken the bullets out of his gun.

A second shot whizzed by, barely missing him as he crashed against the wall and overturned the trash basket beneath the desk. In a flash, Fargo saw his possible salvation. How could he have overlooked it? He reached out and grabbed the few papers in the basket, stuffing them into his shirt as he came to his feet. The marshal's pistol exploded again, catching him on the outside of the thigh, the impact hurling him against the wall. Fargo knew he'd been hit. And bad. But he felt no pain. The pain would come later.

The marshal would kill him right here and now, Fargo realized. He'd have to do what they'd been wanting him to do all along—make a run for it.

Fargo bent his good leg and sprang head-first through the window as a fourth shot shattered the air. His head and shoulders hit the glass and it exploded outward, showering glittering shards. He rolled down the tin roof, over and over, holding his hands protectively over his face and eyes. The arrows of glass cut into his shoulders and back.

Fargo caught the edge of the roof and swung down, dropping to his feet. Another shot passed by overhead. The men shouted with fury at his escape. Or pretended fury, he thought.

Fargo stepped to the pinto and mounted, pulling the reins toward him. The Ovaro whinnied and gathered its legs underneath it, vaulting over the rail fence of the yard and into a dusty street.

Fargo clung to the horse, hunched low as the bullets chased them down the street. He looked about, hoping to see something he recognized. The town, a few lumber buildings huddled together amidst some low buff hills, looked vaguely familiar. Wyoming Territory. Somehow he knew he was in Wyoming, but the rest was a blank. He headed straight down the street toward the edge of town and the wide open country beyond.

Now where the hell would they expect him to run? And how could he keep from going there?

The Ovaro galloped furiously as they passed by the last buildings. Fargo turned about in the saddle to see if he was being pursued.

"Welcome to Bentwood," he read on the sign leading into town. He could see the men running out into the main street toward their tethered horses to pursue him.

He faced forward as the road took a turn and carried him out of sight. He had no doubt another bunch of men were waiting for him somewhere just ahead. His keen eyes scanned the barren hills. He would be trapped between the two groups of men and they would drive him into some deserted spot and shoot him. Or hang him. Or both.

And it wouldn't matter what he said. Or what was the truth. They'd be certain they had found the murderer. And that would be justice enough.

Fargo scanned the hills again, lost in thought. The marshal and the men following were counting on the fact that Fargo would be trying to put as many miles as possible between him and Bentwood. The ambush was sure to be just ahead. Close enough that he would run into it in the first wave of panic. Fargo smiled for the first time all day. That was exactly what he wasn't going to do.

Fargo brought the pinto to a halt and turned it off the road. They plunged down into a sage-choked ravine, out of sight. He dismounted and inspected his thigh. The bullet was imbedded in the muscle toward the outside. He'd been damn lucky. It hadn't shattered the bone or severed his artery, in which case he'd have bled to death in minutes. But the ugly wound was seeping and starting to throb like hell. And the leg hung useless. Whatever he did, he had to have the bullet pulled out right away. And he doubted he could do it himself.

Approaching hoofbeats sounded on the road. Fargo peered out of the thicket as the marshal and the three men swept by in a cloud of dust. He had only a matter of minutes before they discovered he wasn't ahead of them and they turned back to look.

Fargo swung up on the horse. He was beginning to feel the leg now. It wouldn't be long before the pain would be intolerable. He needed to get somewhere safe. Soon. There was no chance he could face down the men. Fargo didn't even bother to look in his saddlebag, since he was sure that whoever had unloaded his Colt had also taken his extra bullets.

The safest place, right now, was the last place they would look for him: right in the middle of the town of Bentwood. Fargo kept the pinto walking through the underbrush beside the road for the short distance back to Bentwood.

At a stand of dead cottonwood, at the edge of town, he slid down. He removed the saddle and bridle from the pinto and hid them in a thicket. He stroked the pinto and the faithful Ovaro nuzzled him. The horse's distinctive black-and-white markings would be a dead giveaway if it was spotted tethered in town. The pinto would be safer running free. And if he needed it, he would whistle. The horse, if it could hear him, would come.

And if he got caught, he'd be damned if he wanted the proud and free Ovaro to end up the stolen property of the marshal or his men. No, the horse was better running free.

"Get on out there," Fargo said quietly to the pinto, slapping its withers gently.

The Ovaro snorted uneasily and took a step, then turned to look back.

"Get," Fargo said again. The Ovaro started out toward the open land reluctantly, turning from time to time to look back at Fargo.

This side of the town seemed quiet, Fargo noted, turning away from the pinto. He'd need a hell of a lot of luck if he was going to stay alive for the next few hours. And luck seemed in short supply on this particular day.

Fargo encircled the town, watching carefully, keeping under cover of the scrub. At the back of one building was a dusty yard. A big yellow dog dozed in the shade and a small garden plot withered under the sun's glare. Just then, a young slender girl in a blue cotton dress emerged from the house carrying a bucket. Sunburnt, with pale blond hair and long, doe-like legs, she seemed to be about sixteen. She walked quickly toward the garden plot and began to carefully pour water on the dispirited plants. She stood facing the house with her back toward Fargo.

This was his chance. It was damned hard to move quickly and silently, dragging one leg behind him, but in a moment, Fargo emerged from the brush and came up behind her. He grasped her suddenly, noting the curved slenderness of her waist. He cupped his other hand over her mouth and pulled her close to him so that he could speak into her ear.

"Just do as I say and you won't get hurt."

She dropped the bucket and struggled in his grasp, trying to bite his hand.

"Easy," he said. "Walk with me to the house. Or else."

The girl continued to struggle for a moment as he held

her tight. Then she seemed to give in. She took a step or two toward the house and then stumbled, pitching forward. Fargo, his wounded leg exploding pain at every step, lost his balance and the two of them tumbled to the ground, rolling over.

Fargo managed to keep his hand on the girl's mouth and his grip on her waist. He staggered to his feet, jerking her roughly. His leg screamed in protest.

"Nice try," he said in her ear, his voice gruff with the pain. "But I've got a gun here. I won't hesitate to use it."

Fargo hated to terrorize the girl, but he doubted she'd ever believe his story. His only chance was to play the role of a murderer on the run, desperate enough to kill anyone who got in his way.

The spirit seemed to go out of the girl and she moved toward the building without another incident. The yellow dog awoke and looked up dolefully as they passed by, but didn't rise or growl. They climbed up the short stairs and Fargo pushed her ahead through the doorway.

Fargo glanced about. They stood alone in a kitchen with a cookstove and a wooden counter. In the corner stood an old table with two mismatched chairs, set with two plates and mugs. Ragged curtains hung at the window. Everything was clean, but he could tell the girl and her family didn't have much money.

"I'm about to take my hand away from your mouth," he said quietly. He drew his pistol, still holding her close with his arm. He jammed the barrel of the Colt just under her ribs and cocked the hammer for effect.

"One word from you and . . . remember what I said," he whispered. It didn't matter that the Colt was empty now, Fargo thought to himself. He wouldn't shoot the girl even if she called out. But she didn't know that.

She nodded, trembling. Fargo slowly took his hand away.

"Who else is at home?" he whispered. "And keep your voice down."

"Nobody," she said. "We're alone."

Fargo jerked her hard against him and she cried out.

"Don't lie to me," he warned her. He had an instinct that someone else was in the house.

"Francine?" a woman's voice called from above.

The girl hesitated.

"Answer her," Fargo said. "Keep it normal. If you tip her off, I'll shoot her."

"Yes, Mother?" Francine called out, trembling.

"I thought I heard you call," the voice said, concerned.

"No. No, everything's . . . fine."

"Very good," Fargo said. "Now, ask her to come down and help you with something."

"I can't," Francine whispered. "She's sick. She hasn't been out of bed since spring."

"That's better," Fargo said. He could tell she wasn't lying. "You keep telling me the truth and everything will be just fine. Anybody else at home?"

Francine shook her head no.

"Let's go up," Fargo said.

She led the way through the small rooms, furnished sparsely and poorly, although everything was well-kept and clean. They climbed the steep stair awkwardly, Fargo leaning heavily on her, favoring his bad leg. The bullet wound was excruciatingly painful now. He ground his teeth as they climbed.

At the top of the stairs, he halted and put a hand out to steady himself until the waves of pain subsided somewhat and he could go on.

"Francine?" the mother's voice called again. "Is that you?"

"I'm . . . coming," the girl said.

They entered a small bedroom with sloping ceilings and an iron bedstead. On it lay a thin pale woman, her hair streaked gray and pulled back from her tired face, etched deep with lines of worry. Her eyes widened and she sat up weakly as her daughter and Fargo entered the room.

"Oh, my God," the woman said. She clasped her hands in front of her. "Please, sir. Please. Do anything you like with me, but please leave my daughter alone. Please, I beg you."

Fargo pushed Francine down on a chair and leaned against the wall. He chewed the inside of his lip to keep the room from whirling crazily around him as the pain radiated up his leg. He noticed the women looking at his torn thigh, and he knew without looking that it had bled all the way down his Levis.

Fargo released the hammer of his Colt and cocked it again, looking over the two women.

"Anybody else in the house?" Fargo asked the sick woman.

She shook her head.

"What's your name?" He pointed the barrel toward her.

"Marilyn Foster," she murmured. Her eyes were wide with fear. Francine slid from her seat and went to sit beside her mother on the bed. The two women held hands as Fargo watched them for a moment.

"Who else lives here?" he asked.

"No one," Francine said quickly.

Fargo pointed the Colt and adjusted his finger along the trigger.

"There were two plates on the table downstairs. And Marilyn doesn't get out of bed. Who else lives here?"

"Tommy," Francine said, her face pale.

"He'll be home from school any moment," Marilyn put in.

"He's my husband," Francine said. "He . . . teaches school. And he's big and he's got a gun. And when he walks in, I'll scream and he'll kill you."

"Nice try," Fargo said. "No wedding ring?"

Francine looked down at her naked fingers and blushed, biting her lip.

Just then, a door slammed downstairs and Fargo heard the sound of running feet.

"Ma! Francie! I'm home!" The voice was that of a young boy.

"Shut the door," Fargo said to Francine. "And do exactly as I say. Otherwise, I'll shoot the kid right between the eyes." He kept his voice low and menacing.

Francine rose and closed the door just as Tommy's footsteps could be heard climbing the stairs.

"Hold it shut," Fargo said, moving beside her so he could whisper his instructions to her.

"Tell him your mother's had a bad attack. Real bad. He can't come in. And to fetch the doctor. Quick. Or else she might die. Got it?"

Francine did as she was told, shouting the instructions to Tommy on the other side of the door.

"Ma? Ma?" Tommy called, his voice scared. "Just hold on, Ma. I'll be right back with the doc!"

Tommy ran down the stairs and out the door, slamming it behind him. Everything was silent for a long moment.

"Good," Fargo said. He pushed Francine toward Marilyn's bed. "Sit over there where I can keep an eye on you both. Now we wait."

Fargo pulled a chair toward him and sank down on it. A thousand Indians were now hatcheting his leg, tearing into it in a thousand painful places and setting fire to his flesh. Once again, he fought the waves of blackness which threatened to drown him.

"How long you been in Bentwood?" Fargo asked the women suddenly. He needed to talk, to keep his mind moving so he wouldn't black out.

"A year," Marilyn said, bitterness in her voice. "Came from Missouri, just in time for the influenza epidemic."

"That what you got?" Fargo asked the sick woman. She shook her head no.

"It killed my dad," Francine said shortly.

Fargo nodded slowly, imagining the two women trying to get by in the rough town without a man in the house. He felt himself relax by slow degrees. He fought it and then holstered his Colt. He could draw it in an instant and wave it about again, if needed.

"You're the one who murdered that girl, aren't you?" Marilyn asked nervously.

Fargo looked at her with narrowed eyes.

"What are you talking about?" he said slowly.

"That girl at the Dusty Rose Saloon . . ." Marilyn's voice trailed off and her face grew even paler, frightened of his reaction.

"What do you know about that?" Fargo asked, anger in his voice.

Marilyn shrugged.

"I said, what do you know?" Fargo repeated, resting his hand on the butt of the holstered Colt.

"Just what I read in the paper," Marilyn said hastily. She

handed a folded newspaper to Francine who hesitantly rose and handed it to Fargo.

Fargo unfolded the newspaper. There on the front page were screaming headlines: DUSTY ROSE DAME DEAD, BRUTAL BUTCHER ON THE LOOSE.

Goddamn it. It had been just over an hour since the marshal and his cronies had burst in on him with the dead girl. And here he was on the front page of the morning newspaper. It didn't make sense. Once again, Fargo wondered when he'd wake up from this nightmare.

He glanced at the story but couldn't read it because the hatchets were hacking again at his thigh and dark undulations clouded his vision, causing the letters of newsprint to jump all over the page. But one thing he couldn't miss. There, in the center of the front page was a drawing of his face, not a very good one. But the dark beard and hair, the deep eyes and strong jaw were unmistakably his.

And underneath was written: $500 REWARD FOR INFORMATION. $2000 DEAD OR ALIVE.

Oh yeah, Fargo thought. He'd been set up. And set up good.

UNTAMED ACTION ON
THE WESTERN FRONTIER

☐ **OUTLAW by Warren Kiefer.** Lee Garland. Since the last Apache uprising made him an orphan child, he's seen it all, done it all, in war, in peace, in the West and East. He's the last great hero in a roaring, rollicking saga that shows how wonderful America is. (169549—$5.99)

☐ **A LAND REMEMBERED by Patrick D. Smith.** Tobias MacIvey started with a gun, a whip, a horse and a dream of taming a wilderness that gave no quarter to the weak. He was the first of an unforgettable family who rose to fortune from the blazing guns of the Civil War, to the glitter and greed of the Florida Gold Coast today. (158970—$5.99)

☐ **THE LEGEND OF BEN TREE by Paul A. Hawkins.** A hero among heroes in a great epic saga of the American West. In the conquered frontier of 1856, Ben Tree is caught between the worlds of the white man and the Indian. He's the last of the mountain men and the first of the gunslingers. (176677—$4.50)

Prices slightly higher in Canada

Buy them at your local bookstore or use this convenient coupon for ordering.

PENGUIN USA
P.O. Box 999 – Dept. #17109
Bergenfield, New Jersey 07621

Please send me the books I have checked above.
I am enclosing $_____ (please add $2.00 to cover postage and handling).
Send check or money order (no cash or C.O.D.'s) or charge by Mastercard or VISA (with a $15.00 minimum). Prices and numbers are subject to change without notice.

Card #_____ Exp. Date _____
Signature_____
Name_____
Address_____
City _____ State _____ Zip Code _____

For faster service when ordering by credit card call **1-800-253-6476**

Allow a minimum of 4-6 weeks for delivery. This offer is subject to change without notice.

By the year 2000, 2 out of 3 Americans could be illiterate.

It's true.

Today, 75 million adults...about one American in three, can't read adequately. And by the year 2000, U.S. News & World Report envisions an America with a literacy rate of only 30%.

Before that America comes to be, you can stop it...by joining the fight against illiteracy today.

Call the Coalition for Literacy at toll-free **1-800-228-8813** and volunteer.

Volunteer Against Illiteracy. The only degree you need is a degree of caring.